# girl
## UNDERCOVER

# NIGHTMARE

Before she could strike, the intruder hurled something at her. Automatically she turned her head aside and held her arms up for protection. It hit her forearm, then clattered to the floor. *Ouch. A metal trowel.*

He scrambled to his feet and bolted for the door.

Jesse dived forward and tackled his legs. He fell, kicked madly. One foot caught her on the side of the face…

Also available in this series

# girl
## UNDERCOVER

# NIGHTMARE

## CHRISTINE HARRIS

■ SCHOLASTIC

Scholastic Children's Books,
Euston House, 24 Eversholt Street,
London, NW1 1DB, UK
A division of Scholastic Ltd
London ~ New York ~ Toronto ~ Sydney ~ Auckland
Mexico City ~ New Delhi ~ Hong Kong

First published in Australia by Omnibus Books,
an imprint of Scholastic Australia, 2005
This edition published in the UK by Scholastic Ltd, 2006

10 digit ISBN: 0 439 95069 4
13 digit ISBN: 978 0439 95069 5

Printed by Nørhaven Paperback A/S, Denmark

10 9 8 7 6 5 4 3 2 1

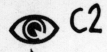 C2

What is this organization?
Who are we working for?
What do they want from us?

Danger!

 Me

Jesse Sharpe.
Who am I?
Do I have a family?
Why does C2 keep me prisoner?

# Rohan

My C2 "brother".
Where is he?
Will I ever see him again?

I miss him.

# Jai

My C2 "brother".
I won't escape without him.
That's a promise

I must protect him.

## Operation IQ

Secret programme run by C2.

Tests, experiments on, and trains prodigies.

Why?

How can we all be orphans?

# What will happen to us?

## Director Granger

New head of C2.

How many secrets does he hide?

### Ruthless.

## Prov

Director's office manager.

Is helping me putting her in danger?

### Help me

## Mary Holt

Carer for IQ children.

Spies on us. Why?

### Like a cobra.

## Liam

My "partner".

Can I trust him?

# Beware!

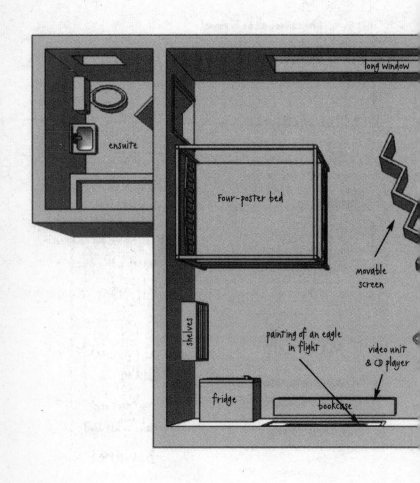

My room — "the fishbow[l]"

long window

ensuite

Four-poster bed

movable
screen

shelves

painting of an eagle
in flight

video unit
& CD player

fridge

bookcase

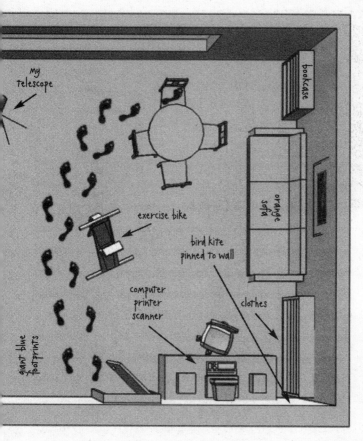

my telescope

bookcase

exercise bike

bird kite
pinned to wall

orange
sofa

computer
printer
scanner

clothes

giant blue
footprints

corridor

# 1

The face was monstrous, distorted. Eyes wider than normal, with a square snout and a long jaw.

Jesse stared. *Creepy*.

It was late and dark. Street lights cast an eerie glow, which made Liam's face mask look sinister.

"We could start a new fashion trend," whispered Liam, his voice muffled.

"If you want to look like a mutant pig." Jesse hoped her own masked face didn't look as weird as Liam's. Although, with his pale, pockmarked skin, crooked nose and tousled hair, Liam would never make a list of most beautiful people.

Still in a crouching position, he pressed the tiny light button on his watch. "Forty-five seconds to go."

Jesse nodded. Her heart beat faster. *What if someone catches us?*

She gave a tiny shrug. In a way, she was already a

prisoner. The secret organization C2 made sure of that. The word prisoner had not occurred to her before. But it was true. Her mind flashed a dictionary definition, *a person or thing confined by another's grasp*. She often wished that she didn't have an extraordinary memory. Then she wouldn't recall things she wanted to forget.

"Gas will be circulating through the air-conditioning system by now. The guards will be falling unconscious. Don't take off your mask till we're out and away." Liam's breathing, inside his own gas mask, sounded strange, exaggerated.

*It's like being on a stakeout with Darth Vader*, thought Jesse.

"Ready?" he asked.

Jesse patted the tiny flash drive that hung on a chain around her neck. Only the size and weight of a pack of chewing gum, it had plenty of space for the files she had to download from the computer. The floor plan was imprinted in her memory, yet hot prickles swept the back of her neck. Even from out here, she didn't like this place. Didn't want to go inside.

"I know what I have to do," she said. "I just don't know *why*."

Liam turned, aiming the chunky nose of his gas mask in her direction once again. "You don't *need* to know why. Jesse Sharpe, you ask too many questions."

2

"I'm a kid. Kids ask questions."

He shook his head. "No. You're a C2 agent. None of us is anything else. We can't be if we want to stay alive. Remember that. Wait ten seconds, then follow." He shot forward, and was immediately absorbed into the darkness.

Jesse tensed, ready to run.

Nervously, she looked up at the illuminated *Cryohome* sign on the roof of their targeted building. They were about to break into a place that froze dead people.

Jesse slipped through the door of Cryohome. She paused to orientate herself, blinking in the sudden electric light.

The body of a security guard was slumped on the floor in front of her. A half-eaten muesli bar lay beside his outstretched fingers. *Don't think about him. Think about what you have to do.* She took a deep breath inside her mask and stepped around the guard.

Jesse held her illuminator tightly in her right hand. If she pressed it, a flash would temporarily blind an opponent, allowing her to escape. This time, the enemy didn't seem capable of attack. But she wasn't taking any chances.

She crossed the cheerfully decorated waiting room with its potted plants and pale lemon walls. Photographs of middle-aged men with too many chins and fake smiles hung above powder-blue sofas. Jesse shivered. Pretty colours could not disguise what this place was really about.

To her left, a dozen C2 agents, menacing in black clothes and gas masks, advanced along the corridor. She sprinted to catch up. Her head pulsed uncomfortably. Perhaps the gas mask was too tight.

More security guards were crumpled throughout the building. A lot of protection for one business.

A man stepped into the corridor directly in front of them.

Jesse flinched. The other agents snapped into "threat" mode, their weapons aimed at the stranger.

The man stood motionless, his arms out from his body to show he was unarmed. Like them, he wore a gas mask. "Right on time."

Liam spoke over his shoulder. "Stand down. It's our contact, Dr Freeman."

The men immediately obeyed.

Dr Freeman looked as though he'd thrown on his clothes in a hurry and almost missed. He wore a wrinkled black T-shirt adorned with a picture of a skull, faded jeans and grubby sneakers. "Jamie" was printed on his name tag.

Jesse felt the man's eyes bore into her. *Take photos. They last longer.*

"Got a pigmy with you tonight?" he chuckled.

Liam tensed. "People who stick their noses where they don't belong get them chopped off."

Was Liam actually defending her? A warm feeling infused Jesse. But it was quickly snuffed out as he spoke sharply. "Jesse. We don't have much time. Concentrate."

*Thanks for nothing, Lawnhead.* Along with the others, she reluctantly followed Dr Freeman into a large room. Tall silver-coloured cylinders were stored there.

Dr Freeman tapped one. "Professor Sawyer's in here. There are three bodies in each. That means you'll have to take them all." He grinned. "How's that for a bargain? Three for the price of one."

Jesse sighed. *What's so funny about stealing three dead bodies?*

In a small office next to the storage room, Jesse switched on the computer. Dr Freeman looked over Jesse's shoulder. She wished he would not stand so close.

"Passwords?" she snapped.

He told her, then warned her of several security traps programmed in for unauthorized users. If she tripped those, the computer would shut down and there was nothing she could do. It was similar to the protection she had put into her own computer back at C2.

"For security reasons, this computer is not connected to any other computer or system," said Dr Freeman.

*Pity*, thought Jesse. Then she could have hacked into Cryohome files from C2 and not had to visit this place with its frozen bodies.

Jesse unclasped the chain around her neck and removed the tiny flash drive. Then she plugged it into the USB port.

"You're obviously good with computers, but aren't there any adults who can do this? Why a kid?"

Jesse shrugged. "I don't cost much."

The mask might obscure Dr Freeman's face, but it didn't hide his interest in her. But she was accustomed to covering her genius, hiding that she was brought up by a secret organization. Officially, she didn't exist. That also meant, if she disappeared, no one would notice. Except her C2 "brother", Jai.

Dr Freeman nodded towards the open doorway and the silver cylinders. "Our guests are not really dead, you know. If we can bring them back to life, then they can't be dead in the final sense."

*Guests? He makes this place sound like a five-star hotel*, she thought, then asked him, "How many have you brought back?"

"Uh … none. Yet. But we're close. The information in those files will show you that. We store the bodies in liquid nitrogen at minus 196 degrees. It's cold enough to stop cell decay. So, they'll keep till we make the breakthrough."

Jesse clicked the mouse and waited as information was downloaded. The pulsing in her head had become a dull ache.

"Professor Sawyer chose whole-body preservation," said Dr Freeman. "You can have your head frozen for a cheaper price. Isolation is performed between the sixth and seventh vertebrae."

"You mean you chop off their heads."

"Crude but accurate."

"Because a brain can easily be damaged, we keep it inside the skull. Our memories, our identity – who we are – is all stored in the brain. When we can re-animate it, but with a new body, then it's the same person. Just whole and healthy."

Storing frozen heads in cylinders didn't seem like happy-ever-after to Jesse, but she didn't argue.

Suddenly a loud siren sounded.

Liam loomed in the doorway. He shouted, "Explain, Freeman."

"I forgot the check-in. Every half hour, the security guards press a hidden button to show everything's OK. Otherwise, the alarm is triggered."

Download complete, Jesse unplugged the flash drive and leaped to her feet.

"We have to get out." Even with his voice distorted by the mask, Dr Freeman sounded frightened. "Where's my money? You promised I'd get it tonight."

Liam flung one arm around Dr Freeman and, with the other, ripped off his gas mask.

# 4

Jesse entered her room on the tenth floor of the C2 building. The curtains were open and the city glowed with lights.

What was that scent? Mary Holt, her carer, might have been snooping again. But that scent was not hers. Mary thought perfumes were unnatural and necessary only if people didn't wash. It wasn't Liam's aftershave. Besides, he had been at Cryohome tonight.

Jesse couldn't place the aroma. She massaged her forehead with two fingertips, then yawned. Her eyes felt gritty. *I'm tired. That's why I can't remember.* Her four-poster bed looked inviting and there were still some hours left to sleep.

Somewhere in the building, Liam and the others were storing the silver cylinder that held the body of the dead professor. She shook her head, warning her thoughts not to stray down that road. Otherwise, no matter how tired she was, she'd never sleep.

When Dr Freeman discovered that he'd been double-crossed, he'd be furious. But what could he do? He thought they were from another agency. People from C2 never told the truth when they could invent a lie.

Jesse sat on the sofa to loosen the laces of her sneakers. Her thoughts drifted to Rohan. He and Jai were like her family, even though they didn't have the same parents. The three of them had been adopted by the secret organization C2. As always, when she remembered Rohan, a pang rippled across her chest. Every day since his disappearance, she had thought about Rohan, worried about what had happened to him.

Then it hit her. That scent was just like Rohan's apple shampoo. Prov, the Director's office manager, had given it to him.

Forgetting her half-untied laces, Jesse stood and looked around her room. She always arranged her belongings carefully, so that if anyone searched through them she would know.

Tonight, however, everything was where it should be: her round table with four chairs; orange sofa; exercise bike; computer desk; shelves for her clothes and books, the telescope. Even her pens were stacked correctly in the holder.

Her eyes turned to the closed door of her bathroom. She found it harder to breathe. Was someone hiding in there? Had Rohan returned and decided to play a trick on her? Adrenalin surged through her, making her heart pound.

She tiptoed to the door, then stopped just short of it. No, Rohan would not be so cruel. Besides, Director Granger said Rohan was sick. Too sick to have visitors or take phone calls. Jesse flung open the door, balancing lightly on both feet, hands up. Accomplished in tae kwon do and karate, she was ready to defend herself.

The bathroom was empty. She stepped back into her bedroom, then froze. The hairs on her arms stood to attention. Without being aware of it, she reached out with one hand.

*Rohan!* Cheeky grin, green eyes, the dimple in his chin and with that funny gap between his two front teeth. It was definitely him. But it was only a face, nothing more, on her computer screen. Then it dissolved – eyes first, then his nose, as though something had eaten them away. Cheekbones, ears, forehead, till there was nothing left.

Unsteadily, Jesse crossed the room and looked under her desk. Just as she'd left it hours earlier, the cord lay neatly coiled on the floor. Her computer was not plugged in.

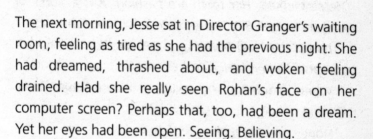

# 5

The next morning, Jesse sat in Director Granger's waiting room, feeling as tired as she had the previous night. She had dreamed, thrashed about, and woken feeling drained. Had she really seen Rohan's face on her computer screen? Perhaps that, too, had been a dream. Yet her eyes had been open. Seeing. Believing.

She felt Prov watching her and pushed the disturbing memory away.

Today Prov wore purple. With her vibrant clothing and swarthy skin, she was not someone you could overlook. Her Italian parents had named her *Providenza*, but she preferred *Prov.* "Short and simple," she sometimes said, "just like me." Although she was short, she was certainly not simple. Beneath her heavy eyeliner and thick lashes, Prov's eyes showed uncertainty.

Jesse wondered if her look meant that Prov knew why

she had been called in. *Maybe I've done something wrong.* Her head pulsed. "Two thousand, two hundred."

"Pardon?"

Jesse spoke louder, "Two thousand, two hundred. The human body contains enough sulphur to make two thousand, two hundred matchheads."

"I see. How did I ever live without knowing that?" Prov's smile revealed teeth that were almost too perfect and white to be real.

Jesse blinked. *Her teeth are flashing. Is it a signal, a secret message? Silly. How could teeth send messages? It's noses that send messages. Pinocchio. Pinocchio's nose grows when he lies.*

"When people lie, a chemical is released that swells the nasal tissues," Jesse said aloud.

"Honey, are you feeling all right?"

"I don't get sick. Jai doesn't get sick. But Rohan is sick. How can that be?" Jesse knew she was babbling, but couldn't stop.

As if a switch had clicked in her mind, her thoughts slowed. The pulsing ceased. Jesse smiled at Prov. "I'm fine. Really."

The inner office door opened. Granger beckoned.

Reluctantly, Jesse followed. Three levels underground, with no windows, his office made her feel confined, surrounded. Prov had brightened up the waiting room with flowers and magazines, but Granger's office lacked colour. *Like him*.

"Sit down, Jesse." The Director adjusted his tie with one hand. Why did he do that? His tie was never crooked. He looked at her with no expression. "Your time of probation has ceased."

Jesse sat rigidly, not daring to move. *Ceased? What does that mean?*

"So far, you have completed your missions successfully. Your palm print and identification details have been programmed into the computer. You are now authorized to leave and enter the building alone."

She released her breath, unaware that she had been holding it.

Granger laced his manicured fingers together. "There will be times when it is necessary for you to accomplish a task on your own. Liam won't always be available to escort you. I recommend you take advantage of this privilege only when necessary. There are cameras in the corridors that record all movement. Wherever you are, we can find you." His voice suddenly softened. "And you know how much we care for you. We, here at C2, are your family."

The only family like this was the Mafia. And comparing them to C2 was like putting a kitten side-by-side with a man-eating tiger.

"We know you won't stray too far." He smiled. "Jai depends on you."

The smile was fake. The threat was real. Granger would hold Jai hostage. Jai would never survive without her. He'd be afraid, lost and without hope. She would never escape without him. Besides, where would she go? She had no family, no friends, no safe place to hide. Although she was now permitted to leave the building on her own, she was just as trapped as before.

Yes, Granger was definitely like a tiger. Mother tigers hid their young in long grass because if the fathers found them, they ate them.

Anger fired inside Jesse. "I want to ask a question."

He inclined his head. "Of course."

"Where is Rohan?"

Granger blinked. "Ah. Poor Rohan. I should have told you before, but I knew it would upset you."

*As if you care.*

"Rohan is dead."

# 6

Jesse pressed her back against the corridor wall. That way, the surveillance cameras might not detect her. Her mouth was dry. Her feet refused to move. If only she could remember where her room was. How long was it since she'd left that office? The man there told her Rohan had died. *That man's nasty. His smile has teeth. Minus 196 degrees. That's another number. A dead number that freezes bodies. Is Rohan minus 196?*

"Hey!" A gruff voice came from behind her.

A tall, pale-skinned man with a massive moustache stood with his hands on his hips. She had seen him before, patrolling corridors and peering behind doors.

*I know what you are. You're a spy. Be careful,* she told herself, *don't let him find out anything.*

The guard frowned. "You know this floor is out of bounds. What are you doing here, kid?" He stalked to her side and grabbed her arm in a firm grip.

Reacting instinctively, Jesse dug her thumb into his radial nerve. His arm fell away, fingers useless. He wouldn't be able to use them till the paralysis wore off.

"You little brat." He grabbed her neck with his other hand, pressing her against the wall. "Calm down." His moustache bounced as he spoke.

*It's alive.*

Jesse aimed a karate chop at the base of his neck. He ducked. She connected with muscle and missed the brachial plexus, the spot that would have rendered him unconscious. He grunted, but retained his grip on her neck.

She lashed out in a frenzy of flailing arms and wild screams. Her fingernails raked the man's face, leaving stripes on his cheek. *Another tiger.*

From behind him, down the corridor, came the sound of running feet. *Tigers are everywhere.*

Suddenly Jesse was surrounded. She was pushed to the ground, held down. *They're going to kill me. You can tell if someone's dead by rubbing a cloth over their eyeballs. If they blink, they're not dead yet.* She screamed, "Don't touch my eyeballs!"

Somewhere in chaos, a male voice boomed out, "This kid's gone crazy."

Leather straps bound Jesse's wrists and ankles to a hospital bed. She lay in the infirmary adjoining the laboratory. Roger, one of C2's scientists, was in the room. And a technician.

She stopped struggling and lay still, eyes closed. Deliberately, she slowed her breathing. If she kept still, they wouldn't focus so intently on her. Then she might be able to escape. *If old cockroaches are decapitated, they're more likely to escape predators.* They run faster.

The skin on her wrists stung where she had tried to pull free of the restraints. Her right leg twitched uncontrollably. Flashes of light illuminated the backs of her eyelids like lightning strikes.

Roger and the technician began whispering.

*Are they talking about pens? I know about pens.* That was another way to find out if victims were dead. You stuck a pen in their throat. If they were alive, they gagged. *I have to listen for pens.*

Ari, the newest member of the medical team, entered the room. Even with her eyes closed, she knew it was him. His right foot was slightly turned in and scraped the floor. Not long ago, he'd defected from his own country to C2. *He didn't know what he was getting into.*

Suddenly Ari was in charge of the laboratory, not Roger. She wondered if Roger resented that, or was he relieved to hand over responsibility? *Maybe he's afraid of them too...*

She felt Ari's fingers touch her wrist, checking her pulse. "Don't worry, Jesse," he said. "I will help you."

*Yeah, right. Help me stop breathing.*

"I know you are awake," he said. "Your eyelids are fluttering."

*Does he know about the tigers?*

Ari said, "Tigers?"

She had spoken aloud. She hadn't realized that.

There was a sharp sting to the back of her hand. Jesse peeked beneath her eyelids. Ari had inserted a needle, and an intravenous tube attached to a machine snaked away from it.

"It will be over soon," said Ari.

Her eyes flew wide open. There was a strange taste on her tongue. Her pulse quickened.

Ari's face seemed to swell, as though he were a pumped-up balloon with eyes. "You helped saved my life, Jesse. Now I am going to save yours."

Jesse pictured a tall, silver cylinder with bodies inside. Then she slid away on a wave of dizziness.

Jesse returned to consciousness but kept her eyes closed. The restraints had been removed from her wrists and ankles. *How long have I been out of it?* Her mind was clear. She felt good, bursting with energy, but kept perfectly still. She wanted to listen to Director Granger and Ari.

"Do you think she'll be all right now?" asked Granger.

"Better than before."

"It was time for an upgrade. I just didn't expect it to happen like this."

*An upgrade? What do they think I am – a computer?*

"She will have to be told," said Ari. "She needs to monitor herself, in case this happens again."

*Told what?* A spear of nervousness shot through Jesse.

"I thought you said it wouldn't happen again," said Granger.

"We should be prepared, just in case."

There was a small silence. "I suppose you're right, Ari."

"Will Jesse be able to handle the truth?"

*The truth? Granger wouldn't know the truth if it jumped up and bit off his nose.* Then Jesse wondered if she was also like that. She had heard so many stories, so many lies. *How do you know when something is true?*

"She is a remarkable and intelligent girl," said Ari.

Granger snorted. "In this case, she can thank us for much of that. I doubt she realizes how lucky she is. Tell her, Ari. But not about the message."

*What message? From Liam or Jai?* As hard as she tried, she couldn't think of any reason a message from either of them would be kept secret.

"When you've sorted out the girl, start on the Professor," said Granger.

Jesse shivered. She hoped neither man had noticed. Then they would know she was eavesdropping. She had a strong suspicion that Granger's "Professor" was the dead body they had retrieved from Cryohome.

# 9

The smell of hot chocolate made Jesse's stomach rumble.

"Jesse." Ari's voice intruded on her daydream. "Your eyelids are fluttering again."

She opened her eyes. Granger had gone.

"Here." Ari held out a mug of steaming chocolate. "Your carer, Mary Holt, is not here. If you drink this I will not tell. Not even under torture."

In C2, even when people were joking – which wasn't often – they spoke about "torture". Did normal people do that? Jesse didn't think so.

The scar on Ari's left eyelid moved as he smiled. His manner was warm and friendly. But what would he have done if Granger had forbidden him to help her?

Jesse sat up and took the mug of chocolate. The strong aroma made her slightly dizzy. She took a sip. *Mmm. Delicious.* She hoped Ari hadn't made it in a test tube out the back of the laboratory.

He grabbed a chair and sat beside her. "I do not know how much of my conversation with the Director you heard, but I suspect you have questions."

Silently, she eyeballed Ari through the steam rising from her chocolate. *Never reveal how much you know.*

"Have you heard of nanotechnology?" Ari didn't wait for her to answer. "You have... When you were a toddler, you were injected with nanites, sub-microscopic machines. They are so small even a microscope will not pick them up. A dot on a page would equal a million nanoscale devices."

"Injected? Why?"

"Think of nanites as microscopic submarines. They were programmed by computer to reach your brain and release a chemical which stimulates activity. It made you smarter."

Suddenly queasy, Jesse handed Ari back the unfinished chocolate. She had often wondered how people from C2 knew she was a prodigy when they rescued her from the car crash that killed her parents. She had been only two years old. "So I'm not really a genius?"

"Indeed you are. Your abilities are far greater than usual in someone your age. You must know that. There are your skills with languages and music. Your extraordinary memory."

"But I wasn't born that way."

He put the mug of chocolate down on a cupboard. "Is anyone? Experts have debated for years about whether people are gifted from birth or develop their abilities afterwards."

"I'm artificial."

"You are simply enhanced. Like people who wear glasses to improve their vision or an aid to boost their hearing."

"But they can take off their glasses or remove the hearing aid. I can't do that, can I?" Heat flushed Jesse's face. "I'm a freak!"

"No!" said Ari. "You simply have a super brain."

"Super? What's so good about that? Superman was lonely. He couldn't show people who he really was. I don't want to be a super girl! I just want to be a girl." Jesse didn't care that Superman wasn't a real person. It didn't matter. She'd made her point. Right now, she didn't feel real either.

Her voice rose. "Take those nano-things out of me. Now."

"It is impossible," said Ari. "When these experiments began, this technology was new. The brain…"

"You mean *my* brain."

He nodded. "Yes, and those of other children in Operation IQ. The brain adapted so well to the chemical that it needs it to function."

A growing horror grabbed Jesse. "What if I don't have it any more?"

"There is no gentle way to tell you this, so I will be direct. You would go insane. Probably, in time, you would die."

*I'm hooked. I can never escape.* Clenching her fists, she embedded her fingernails in her palms. If she concentrated on the pain, she might control her emotions.

"Do not give up hope. Research continues. This is my area of specialty. This is why your organization wanted my skills. I flushed the old nanites from your system. You now have the latest, superior technology."

*So that's what Granger meant by "upgrade". Great. So I have the latest model machines digging into my brain.*

"Don't look back," Ari said. "Look forward."

*Easy for you to say. No one mucked with your brain.* But Jesse knew that although Ari's brain might be untouched, his life was not. Back in his home country, Ari had a wife and children whom he could not contact since he defected.

His face softened. "On the positive side, you are useful, valuable. People do not throw away what they value."

It wasn't that simple. Couldn't C2 wipe her out any time and make more geniuses?

27

"I suggest that you keep this information between you and the boy Jai. He should be told. But there are some who would use your abilities for evil purposes," warned Ari.

Jesse hoped that was not happening already at C2. The Director was ruthless. What if he ordered her to do something bad and she refused? Would he have the nanites reprogrammed to stop delivering the chemical her brain needed? *What a choice. Obey and stay sane. Or refuse and turn into a vegetable.*

It was the rats' hearts that disturbed Jesse the most. Plus their connection to the body in the silver cylinder.

Alone in her room, Jesse sat at her computer desk. A chair was propped underneath the handle of her locked door to stop anyone coming in unexpectedly. Mary had her own key and sometimes used it.

Jesse's internet and email connections were re-routed around the world so that nothing could be traced to her. If anyone tried, as soon as the electronic search reached London, there would be a warning message that a virus had infected the computer. If the person ignored that and pursued her electronically to the next stop, New York, it would not simply be a warning. A computer "bug" would back-trace to the source.

Jesse looked at the screen. There were lots of websites on nanotechnology. Scientists were working on tents that might repair themselves. And "smart" army uniforms that they hoped would change colour or manipulate light so as to be invisible. They were experimenting with uniforms that altered from a sleeve to a splint if a soldier broke a limb, and others that monitored a soldier's location or had radio communications woven into the fabric.

*Weird. But not too weird.*

In medicine, scientists hoped to use nanites to break up blood clots, clear arteries or diagnose illnesses.

*Sounds reasonable.*

But the experiment with the rats' hearts was unsettling. A female scientist had frozen rats' hearts in liquid nitrogen for close to an hour. The hearts stopped beating. They were dead. Then the woman re-started them.

Somewhere in the C2 building Professor Sawyer's body was also frozen in liquid nitrogen. Even with special anti-freeze liquid in his veins instead of blood, there would be cell damage. Dr Freeman had talked about re-animation, bringing those bodies back to life. That couldn't happen unless the damaged cells were repaired.

In the infirmary, Granger had told Ari, *When you've sorted out the girl, start on the Professor.*

Jesse knew exactly what they planned for Professor Sawyer. The files she'd downloaded at Cryohome would give the C2 scientists information on the research done so far into what they called "re-animation". But there was still the problem of how to repair cell damage caused to a frozen body by being thawed. C2 was going to use nanotechnology for that. The nanites were so small that they could get *inside* cells. The C2 scientists had already used nanotechnology to turn ordinary children into geniuses. Now they were going to use it to turn a dead body into a live one.

# 11

Jai sat opposite Jesse at the table in her room. He reached across the Chinese Checkers board and jumped a blue marble over three of her red ones.

Jesse noticed, once again, the thinness of his wrists. Sometimes she teased him by saying that they were the same width as sparrow legs. His cheekbones stood out as though he didn't eat enough. But he did. Mary Holt made sure of that. Either Jai was genetically coded to be dainty or he worried away body fat.

He moved the board a fraction to the right. Objects had to be centred. "You have something to tell me."

Jesse hesitated. What she had to say would hurt Jai, worry him. Not long ago, in this same room, he had told her that he was afraid the children in Operation IQ were flawed. That they would break down. Jai had a brilliant mind, but he was only nine years old.

"It is your move." He waited with both hands pressed flat to the table.

She selected the closest red marble. It was not a good choice.

"You are highly intelligent and determined," said Jai. "Yet your mind often drifts when we play games."

"That's OK." She shrugged. "You like to win."

"So do you. That is why I know you have something to tell me." Jai smiled gently. "You have been absent for several days. You could have been on an outside assignment. But I heard whispers that you were ill." He moved another blue marble, jumping from his end of the board to Jesse's.

"Yes, I was sick. Sort of."

"Sort of?"

Deep in this place of lies, she wanted honesty between her and Jai. She told him everything – her hallucinations, memory blanks, strange thoughts, and the wild fears that turned her knees to jelly. Listing her symptoms was the easy part. She had to tell him why it happened. Ari thought it might be better if Jai heard the news from her.

As Jai listened, the colour in his face receded.

Jesse kept her suspicions about Professor Sawyer to herself.

"Did Ari say why C2 chose children like us for this nanotechnology enhancement?" asked Jai.

"No. Maybe it's because kids have fresh, quick minds. Even normal kids learn a lot in a short time. How to walk, talk, sing, recognise shapes, all kinds of things."

Jai nodded. "And we were taken before we formed solid memories. We were too young to say no."

"Neither of us had relatives who would complain. And Operation IQ was an experiment. They wouldn't experiment on themselves. It might go wrong."

The look in Jai's eyes said *It has.*

"Or C2 wanted kids as special agents. The day I met Liam, Granger told him that children are overlooked. People don't really see them. He said, 'That's what we need. Someone who is watching, but doesn't stand out.'"

"That is logical." Jai's tone was flat, dispirited.

Jesse understood his feelings, shared them. She reached out and touched his hand. "I won't give up till we're free of this place. Free of the nanites. Believe me, Jai."

He nodded slowly. "I believe you mean what you say. However, I do not know if it is possible."

"Look at how their technology has improved since they began the experiment on us."

"But Jesse, we are still dependent on the chemical."

"If they could find a way to introduce a chemical to make us smarter, they can find a way to stop it. We just have to be patient. That reminds me … Jai, did you send me a message when I was sick?"

"No." He shook his head. "There is something else you have not told me. It is about Rohan. When you think about him, you look as though you are about to cry. Yet you never cry."

*Everyone cries.*

"What I have to tell you will make you sad," she said. "Rohan won't be coming back."

"He escaped?"

"In a different kind of way."

"He is dead." Jai's voice was faint, almost a whisper.

"Yes. Granger told me. He gave no details. Ari wasn't here when Rohan disappeared. Maybe his nanites broke down, like mine, and they didn't know how to fix him. I don't know. I'm just guessing."

Jai shivered. He withdrew his hand from hers, then moved a blue marble on the board as though there had been no interruption. "It is a dangerous game we are playing."

She knew he wasn't talking about checkers. And it was no game.

# 12

Jesse sat in the briefing office opposite a painting of purple flowers that disguised a computer screen.

Director Granger placed a folder marked *Eyes Only* on the table. "As usual, read, memorize, then leave the folder with Prov. Be ready at eight in the morning. Liam will drop you off. For most of this assignment you will work alone. It should take only a couple of days. If you have any queries, ask Liam."

He left the room without saying goodbye. The smell of his aftershave lingered. Its strong spiciness made her eyes water.

Partly curious, partly reluctant, Jesse opened the folder.

She was going to Watercress Camp. It sounded more like a salad ingredient than a mission. She was to infiltrate a camp of kids about her own age. They had all won places in a science writing competition. The camp was their reward.

*Other kids*. Jesse felt a stirring of excitement. A camp was such a normal thing to do. Except it probably wasn't normal to spy on the others.

There was a plan of the grounds. Although it was in a suburb, the central building was surrounded by a huge garden. High fences marked the borders and, at night, dogs were let loose to guard the property.

Her cover name was *Ellie Saunders*. She liked that. It felt comfortable. Her imaginary mother was sailing around the world on a solo yacht race, while her father was supposed to be a dentist. That explained why a mother would run away to sea.

She continued reading. There were two people she had to locate. The first, a middle-aged man, was a C2 agent working undercover. His name was George. It probably wasn't his real name, but it was easy to remember. A photograph showed him as thin, balding, with a comb-over that looked plastic. His eyebrows bushed into each other over bloodshot eyes. *Where do they get these guys? The ugly shop?*

The notes did not say what was supposed to happen when they met. *Typical C2*. Each person knew only what was essential. That way, if they were captured, they could not be forced to tell the whole plan. Only the little they knew. She didn't want to dwell on how enemies might "force" her to tell.

There was no name or description for the other target. Just that it was a child. An agent under deep cover codenamed "Seahorse" reported that a "child with unusual skills" would be placed at the camp by a group called Nimbus. Was this child another genius like her and Jai? A stray from Operation IQ?

Seahorse did not specify whether the target was a boy or girl, or why these Nimbus people were involved. Only that this child was some kind of threat.

*What does that mean? Couldn't Seahorse have found out more? Or had something happened to him before he could investigate further?*

When Jesse pinpointed the target, she was to contact Liam. The notes did not say what would happen then. She shifted uncomfortably in her chair. Several outcomes came to mind. She did not like any of them.

# 13

Jesse checked her reflection in the side mirror of Liam's car. She almost didn't recognise herself with the carrot-coloured wig and green contact lenses. The sparkle jeans and brown T-shirt were pretty cool as well.

Liam accelerated and Betsy shot forward.

Jesse had no idea why Liam had nicknamed his car Betsy. Although it kind of suited her. The bodywork was rough, but hidden in the glovebox was a small computer screen. And under the bonnet was a deluxe motor that could get them out of trouble in a hurry. Once an assassin's bullet had shattered the back window. Now it was fixed. She and Liam were alive. It could have been worse.

Jesse glanced over her shoulder. "Tidied up a bit?"

"You noticed."

"Yeah, I noticed you threw the rubbish from the front into the back."

"That attitude come with the hair, thumb sucker?"

"I've always had attitude."

She waited for a snappy reply, but he was silent.

"Why are you cranky? You ate breakfast today."

He snorted. "Who said I had breakfast?"

"Cornflakes with soy milk."

"How do you know that?"

*I also know you cleaned your teeth with spearmint paste.*

"You left some on your chin," she said.

He rubbed his face with one hand. "Saves me bringing lunch."

Jesse turned and looked out the side window. There had been nothing on Liam's chin. Her certainty about his breakfast puzzled her.

She tested her sense of smell by taking in a deep breath. *Pizza supreme, hotdog, smelly sneaker, banana peel.* Then she turned her head to check out the mess in the back of the car. *Hah. Pizza container and one shoe.* She'd bet the banana peel and hotdog wrapper were there too, underneath all the other rubbish.

"Something wrong?"

"No. Just checking we're not being followed."

"You might need to look out the window for that. Not at the floor."

A long silence stretched between them.

"OK,' said Jesse. "You have a question on your face that isn't making it to your lips. What is it?"

"I heard you attacked another agent. Is that true?"

"Attacked?" She glared at Liam. "If somebody grabs you around the throat and you fight back, would you call that attacking?"

The car cruised past several restaurants. *Garlic, tomato and oil.* Her sense of smell was so refined, she could distinguish each element. Was this something to do with the updated nanites that fed her brain?

"I heard you went crazy. Gouged his face."

"I was sleepwalking. Had a nightmare where I was being attacked by tigers. He shouldn't have grabbed me."

*The whole situation is one huge nightmare.*

Even if she was permitted to tell Liam what really happened, she would not do it. On their first assignment he told her about a boy from Operation IQ who "...went nuts, turned into some whacko who stayed in his room making models out of lollipop sticks." She clearly remembered Liam adding, "Don't go nuts on me, will you? You could get us both killed."

Back then, Liam had looked at her as though she had two heads. He was doing it again now.

# 14

For the first time, Jesse was partially comforted by C2's fanatical secrecy. What if someone tried to reprogramme her nanites or turn them off? Jesse felt more vulnerable than ever before. Her mind was her strength, yet also her weakness. Enough. *Think about something else.*

"You didn't send me a message in the last few days, did you?" she asked Liam.

"No."

*OK, I give up.* She had no clue what message Granger wanted to hide. *And everyone thinks I'm the one with the head problems!*

Eager to change subjects, she asked, "What is Nimbus?"

Liam clenched his jaw. Either he didn't like the question or he didn't like Nimbus. "They are an underground group who claim to be restoring 'light to a darkened world'. You know what a nimbus is – a circle of light.

Their operations are secret. Every so often they surface, inflict damage on innocent people, then weasel back to their headquarters. Wherever that is. They're bad dudes. They'll use any means to accomplish their goals. And I mean any."

"So they're like C2?"

Liam indicated to turn a corner. "Worse. If you tangle with Nimbus, be really careful, Jesse. I *mean* it."

"I hear you." She sneaked a look at him. He sounded as though he cared about her safety. *Let's not get too warm and fuzzy here, she told herself. Maybe he only wants the mission to succeed.*

Liam checked behind, then parked alongside the kerb. "I'm hungry enough to eat a horse and chase the jockey. I'm nipping into this shop."

"But you ate breakfast."

"So? I ate breakfast yesterday, too. It's worn off."

He added something else, but she didn't focus on the words. It was only static – background noise. Something outside on the footpath held her attention. A sick taste began at the back of her throat.

Liam raised his voice. "Hey! I said, *do you want anything?*"

"Sorry. No. I was daydreaming."

He closed the car door then strode across the footpath.

Jesse continued to stare. An advertisement for the daily paper had been placed on a board. "LEADING SCIENTIST JAMIE FREEMAN KILLED IN FREAK ACCIDENT."

A jolt of fear ran through her. Dr Freeman had helped them steal a body from Cryohome and download secret files from the computer. Now he was dead.

Her last memory of Jamie Freeman was his shocked expression as Liam ripped off his gas mask. Liam had told her that Freeman would wake up when the gas wore off. Was that another lie? Had Liam killed Dr Freeman? As soon as she started to trust Liam, something happened to make her suspicious again. *What would Liam do*, she thought, *if he was ordered to kill me?*

# 15

Jesse paused on the dingy veranda of the old house. She pushed thoughts of Dr Freeman to the back of her mind. For now, she had to concentrate on her mission. *Suspect everyone, believe nothing, watch your back,* Liam had taught her. *A slip of concentration could be a slip to your death.*

The sign beside the door said, "Welcome to Watercress Camp."

Out of sight, to her left, dogs barked. Jesse tensed, ready to run. The barking brought back vivid memories of crashing through the bush with vicious dogs right behind her. Those other dogs had been trained to kill and she had been their target. But today, no dogs ran towards her. They were either locked up or chained.

She sighed with relief and took a long look at the old house in front of her. It resembled a film set from a horror movie. Constructed of grey stone, it had two storeys lined with grimy windows. A creeper snaked up the veranda railing and across one side of the house. Small stone gargoyles with twisted faces crouched beneath the guttering.

Jesse hitched her favourite backpack further up her shoulder. There were lots of scuff marks on it now, besides the ones Liam had made with his boots. "It looks too new," he'd said. *Yeah, right.* He might have been correct, but he shouldn't have enjoyed stomping on it.

Young voices drifted from the open windows of the building. A spark of excitement ignited inside her. Maybe this mission wouldn't be so bad after all.

Jesse knocked on the door.

It opened quickly. A large woman in her fifties blocked the doorway.

"Welcome, my dear." The woman's high-pitched, breathy voice didn't fit her ponderous body. She wore a pink frilly apron over a loose floral dress. The casual clothes didn't work with her thick makeup. Even a layer of pink foundation couldn't hide the open pores on her skin. Her dark eyebrows were thick and straight.

Jesse detected lavender talcum powder over perspiration.

"I'm Daisy," said the woman. "And you are?"

"Ellie Saunders," said Jesse.

Daisy stepped back.

Rustling up a friendly smile, Jesse entered the wide hallway. Her mind raced at sonic speed. She had not met this woman before, yet something about her was familiar. Jesse could not imagine forgetting someone this size. Her feet were like skateboards without the wheels.

She ran through images of faces in her memory. Found one. Stopped. Her mind moved past it. Reversed. *It can't be. Can it?*

Jesse looked Daisy straight in the eyes. Yes, Daisy knew who she was. And she knew that Jesse recognized her. Take away the dress, the frilly apron, the wig and body padding, and there would be a skinny man with a comb-over.

# 16

Daisy rested one hand lightly on Jesse's shoulder, turning her to face into a large room to their right. "This is Ellie Saunders, everyone."

Instinctively, Jesse scanned the room, counted ten boys, seven girls and checked for weapons.

She relaxed. You goose. *This is a camp for kids.* Although she did not relax completely. Things here were not as they seemed on the surface. The overweight woman who greeted her at the door was actually a skinny man. And a secret agent. Besides, one of these kids was a threat of some kind. Whatever that meant. Jesse suspected she would fit that label herself.

Her nose told her they had recently consumed cordial and cheese.

A girl with short hair and pink braces came forward. "Hi. I'm Tracy. We're sharing a room upstairs."

*Sharing?* It could be fun, yet it would complicate

matters if Jesse had to sneak out at night.

Some of the children waved. Others called, "Hello." Two simply stared.

"What was your project about?" asked Tracy. "The one that got you a place here?" Morsels of cheese clung to her braces.

"Lepidoptera."

A plump boy with vivid blue eyes said, "Moths and butterflies."

Tracy glared at him. "Grant. Don't show off. He's from my school. Thinks he knows everything."

*Maybe he does.* Jesse looked at him more closely. Did normal kids know facts like that? "Seahorse" had not specified intelligence in the target child, just a special ability. But what else could it be?

"Yes. It's moths and butterflies."

Tracy clapped her hands. "Cool. What's the best thing you found out about them?"

Jesse shuffled the information she had read the previous night through her memory banks. *The moth that drinks cattle tears? No. The vampire moth, which sucks mammal blood? A bit too much.* "The sphinx moth from Madagascar has a proboscis that's 35 centimetres long."

"Gross." Tracy pulled a face.

"Not really," said Jesse. "It needs to reach the nectar in the bottom of deep orchids."

"But doesn't its pro ... tongue thing catch on trees when it flies?"

"It curls up like a spring."

Tracy did not look impressed. "I did snowflakes."

Daisy detached her hand from Jesse's shoulder and waded into the centre of the room. "OK. You have an hour or so till the first activity begins. Why don't you all go outside and catch some lovely sunshine?" Her voice was soft and cheerful. "Please stay within the gates. Don't walk on the garden beds. And do not approach the dog compound. You will return minus fingers."

"Gross." Tracy paled. That word seemed to be her favourite.

Jesse waited for someone to comment on Daisy's appearance, to guess she was in disguise. But no one did. At least they didn't show it.

"Is that backpack all you brought?" asked Tracy.

Jesse nodded.

"I brought two suitcases. I couldn't decide what to bring, so I packed some of everything."

*So she hasn't planned a quick getaway*, thought Jesse.

"I'll get you some cheese in case you're hungry."

"Thanks."

Tracy was a born organizer. Jesse didn't mind. It left her free to watch the others as they filed past.

A short, thin boy turned towards the stairs instead of the front door. "I have to get a mask," he whined. "Who knows what I could breathe in out there? All those flowers." A blob of green mucus hung from his nostril.

*Too late.*

Grant, scowling and perspiring, drew level with Jesse. "That kid's asthmatic. His project was on germs." He leaned closer. "Want to know what mine was?"

*Not really*, said her head. "Sure," said her voice.

The aroma of second-hand cheese wafted as he spoke. "Praying mantis. It is the only insect with eyes that turn 180 degrees." There was a malicious glint in Grant's eyes. "A praying mantis grabs its victim with pincer-like forelegs." He pinched Jesse's forearm between two fingers. "The mantis bites its victim's neck. Paralyses it. Then it starts eating. While the victim is still alive."

"Let go of my arm." Jesse sent him a withering stare.

He faltered and immediately let go.

Tracy bustled back with cubes of cheddar cheese on a serviette. "You're full of hot air, Grant. One day someone's going to bust your chops. Ignore him, Essie."

"My name's Ellie."

"Sure. Whatever. Let's go."

Jesse followed Tracy to the foot of the stairs. She looked up and stopped. Her breath caught in her throat. Everything seemed to move but her. Dust motes danced on the sunlight streaming in through the skylight. Sneakers scuffed on wooden floorboards and voices faded as the other kids trooped outside. Jesse knew she was staring, but couldn't help it.

A boy stood at the top of the stairs. He had a dimple in his chin and green eyes. If he smiled, there would be a gap between his two front teeth.

Jesse bit her lip to stop herself calling out his name – Rohan.

# 17

"Cute, isn't he?" Tracy's voice cut across Jesse's trance-like stare.

Jesse agreed. Although she wasn't thinking "cute" at that moment. She was thinking "dead."

"Do you know him?"

"He reminds me of ... of my brother," said Jesse.

The boy descended the rest of the stairs two at a time, drawing level with the girls. His eyes met Jesse's. There was no sign of recognition. Nothing. He wasn't pretending or covering up. He simply didn't know her. OK, she was wearing a wig and green contacts. But Rohan would have recognized her. They grew up together.

"Hi." The boy looked puzzled at the girls' attention on him.

"Hi yourself. I'm J ... Ellie Saunders." Jesse forced a smile. Her face felt stiff.

The boy's yellow T-shirt had a logo over his heart,

with the words *Branwood School*. "I'm Peter K-Keaton."

Jesse felt her hopes smash into little pieces. She had heard this boy's soft stutter before, on the telephone. She had seen him, too. But only from a distance, on a bus. Up close like this, he was so much like Rohan, she found it difficult to believe it wasn't him.

She flicked a look at the hand he rested on the balustrade. There was no scar on his forefinger. Rohan had had a scar there from the age of five. Jesse knew that for a fact because she was the one who had pushed him. She had also been the one who held his other hand when he had stitches.

There were other, subtle differences. His hair was longer than Rohan's and he had a side part. The C2 technicians often shaved Rohan's head so that they could attach electrodes for tests. His thick hair got in their way. *Broke the connection*, they said. But even when he did grow his hair, he never parted it. He thought it made him look goofy.

But this boy was too much like Rohan for it to be simple chance. It was not possible. Several explanations jumped into Jesse's mind. He could be a clone or an identical twin.

"What was your project about, Peter?" Tracy's voice was loud and overly enthusiastic. She was trying to get his attention.

54

"Identical t-twins."

Jesse kept her face blank, but her whole body tingled as though electricity was running through her. "Are you a twin?"

"No. Yes."

Tracy giggled.

"That's two answers. I only want one." Jesse smiled at Peter. She didn't want him to feel anxious or cornered. If he did, he might clam up and tell her nothing.

"I was a twin, but my b-brother died at b-birth."

Jesse smiled again, to show she understood how hard it must be to talk about something like that. *Your brother might be dead. But he didn't die at birth.*

Did Rohan have parents out there in the suburbs? Peter was living with someone. If so, that meant Rohan had not been an orphan who needed adoption. He had been kidnapped.

# 18

Late that afternoon, Jesse stood at the kitchen sink peeling potatoes. Daisy bustled confidently around the kitchen. Jesse made herself keep thinking of Daisy as "she" not "he" in case she accidentally broke her cover.

Jesse imagined Liam completing an assignment where he had to cook for more than twenty people while wearing body padding and a dress. *I'd like to see that.*

Tracy chopped carrots. Kids wandered in and out of the kitchen, pinching food and sticking their fingers into the dessert.

Daisy shooed them out. "Tea will be ready sooner if you stop interrupting."

Jesse ran a kaleidoscope of images from the day through her mind. They had all tried the flying fox, obstacle races, sprints, all sorts of activities. During all of that, was there anyone who stood out as especially brilliant or strange?

*They're all strange. Even me. But none of them seems suspicious.*

Several times, Jesse had deliberately fumbled so that no one would suspect that she could do much better. The afternoon was easy compared to her exercise regime at C2. The hardest part was keeping her wig on straight.

One awkward moment came when Tracy asked to borrow Jesse's lip balm. It was actually a concealed camera. She had it so that she could email photos back to C2 if she couldn't identify the target. Maybe someone there would recognize an imposter.

"Uh ... better not," said Jesse. "I get really bad cold sores on my lips and they spread up my face."

Tracy stepped backwards. Her lips formed the letter "G" to say her favourite word – *gross* – but she held back.

A few people stood out for one reason or another. But nothing that would be of interest to C2. There were Tahlia and Bob, the activity supervisors. Tahlia's curves strained the seams of her tracksuit, which looked a size too small. When she moved, there was a whiff of coconut oil. Bob did not simply strain his tracksuit. He *bulged* out of it. His arms and legs were mountains of muscle. Had they wandered off the stage of a "Perfect Body" competition by mistake?

Peter didn't talk much, and he constantly checked his watch.

Grant's favourite word for the afternoon was "Boring." Pale and overweight, he didn't look as though he was into exercise at all.

At first, Jesse had tried to cheer him up. Maybe he wasn't really bored, just worried that he couldn't keep up. "You might be really good at it," she said.

"I'm good at everything," he'd sneered. "What I don't get is why did they send a bunch of smart kids like us to a camp run by steroid munchers?"

Anyone who was genuinely clever wouldn't need to tell everyone. If they had a prize for the sourest expression, Grant would have won. No competition.

Priya had a sharp wit. She had a quip for everything. But Priya was as uncoordinated as a blind giraffe with eight legs.

Ibrahim had outstanding upper body strength. He hung on to the flying fox when everyone else ended up in the creek with wet feet. But Ibrahim was scared of heights. He trembled so violently that he rattled the equipment.

Yingbao ran fast. Jesse was tempted to check his feet for batteries. But when he jumped over obstacles, he kept clipping his toes and falling forward like a tired horse.

Jerome wore a cotton mask. Till he began to hyperventilate.

Tahlia forced his fingers away from the strings of the mask and slid it over his head. "Don't argue. You need fresh air."

Jerome stormed back to the house to get his puffer.

"He's the kind of kid who'd sneeze on his mum when he's eating crackers," said Priya.

Jesse thought about each of them and still had no clue to the identity of the Nimbus infiltrator.

Tracy left the kitchen. The drift of food pickers stopped.

The roar of the blender jolted Jesse back to the present. She looked over at Daisy. So far, there had been no chance to talk.

With a small movement of her head, Daisy indicated that Jesse should come closer.

Jesse checked over her shoulder. The noise should cover their conversation from eavesdroppers. But they had to be careful.

"Meet me at the summer house at ten tonight," said Daisy.

Jesse had seen it that afternoon. A rundown, octagonal building with lattice-work, overgrown with climbing roses. It was far enough from the house to give them privacy.

Daisy met her eyes. "Don't be late. They let the dogs out at eleven. And they haven't eaten all day."

*Great. Do I have a sign on my forehead that says* "Canine lunch"?

"You have a message for me?" asked Jesse.

"No, kiddo. You have one for *me*. You just don't know it yet."

# 19

Tracy was an elephant. An elephant with skateboard knee pads. No, arthritis.

"Elephantiasis," shouted Ibrahim.

Jesse applauded, along with the others. Tracy's contortions were bizarre. But Ibrahim guessed the correct answer. *Elephantiasis, disease marked by huge enlargement of the legs.* What sort of word was that for an after-dinner game of charades? *Too weird.*

She looked across at Peter. He seemed distracted, fidgety. He stood, then eased backwards towards the open doorway and slipped from the room.

Jesse checked her watch. Eight-thirty pm. Still an hour and a half before she was to meet Daisy in the summer house. She followed Peter into the hallway and listened. The games room had gone quiet. Someone was making an idiot of himself again.

Faint sounds ahead drew her to the kitchen. The room

was dark, except for the faint glow from the microwave clock.

Jesse flicked the light switch.

Peter stood motionless by the back door, like a rabbit caught in headlights.

"Sorry," said Jesse. "Did I startle you?"

He flung one hand to his chest. Red colour flooded his cheeks. "I c-came out to get a d-drink. I was thirsty."

She nodded. "It's stuffy in there. All that laughing uses up oxygen."

If he was after a drink, then he was looking in the wrong place. The taps and the fridge were on the other side of the kitchen. Besides, there were jugs of iced water in the room he had recently left. Their eyes met. She saw the exact second he realized that too.

"I w-was sick of w-water."

"Me too." She waited. If the silence grew, he would feel the need to fill it. He might reveal more than he intended.

He shifted from one foot to the other. "F-fish drink water."

She grinned. "They also eat their own droppings."

Peter giggled. It was a high-pitched, girly kind of giggle. Not one Jesse would have imagined coming from a stocky boy like him.

He cleared his throat and headed for the fridge. "D-do you want an orange juice?"

"OK. Oranges should be safe."

Another giggle came from inside the fridge as he took out a large carton with a picture on the side of unnaturally bright oranges.

Jesse chose two glasses from the dish rack. If she was going to wheedle any information from him, it had better be now. Soon the charades game would finish and everyone would be herded upstairs to sleep.

"Do you remember your twin brother?" she asked. "You were together for nine months before you were born."

Peter's hand shook, making him splash some juice. "S-sorry."

She grabbed a sponge and mopped up the spill. "Doesn't matter. I'm the world's biggest klutz. I'm always spilling things or knocking them over."

He took a long sip of his juice. Either he truly was thirsty or he was giving himself time to think. "I d-don't remember my brother. I was t-too young."

"I read in a magazine that most people don't really remember clearly till they have the language to talk about what they've experienced. But I thought you might have a sense of someone else."

He shook his head.

"We have twins in our family," said Jesse. "Does your mum have a photo of your brother?"

Peter tensed. His shoulders rose as the muscles contracted. "My m-mother died. I'm adopted."

Pins and needles zipped across Jesse's skin. *Adopted? Just like Rohan.*

"I also read in that magazine about these twins who were separated at birth and didn't know about each other." She looked at Peter. "They met up by accident when they were fifty years old. Everyone got a shock at how much alike the brothers were. They even lived in the same city. Both played trombone, had joined amateur theatre groups, read the same kind of books, and they both hated catching buses."

Peter's fingers twitched. If he gripped his glass any tighter, it might shatter. He looked aside, clunking the glass down heavily on the cupboard. "I'm t-tired. I'm going upstairs."

"See you tomorrow," Jesse called cheerfully.

The moment Peter left the kitchen, Jesse's smile faded. *No matter how hard he tried, Peter's emotions showed clearly on his face, she thought. He knows about Rohan. Or he's hiding a secret that scares him spitless.*

Jesse lay in the dark listening to the sounds of Tracy's breathing. It had slowed, become quiet and gentle. Her nose made popping noises.

Tracy could talk underwater with a mouthful of marbles. For a while there, it seemed that nothing would stop her but anaesthetic. Finally, Jesse pretended to be asleep and Tracy subsided.

Jesse checked her watch. It was time to leave for the summer house.

Easing back the covers, alert to signs of Tracy stirring, Jesse got up. She was already dressed in black stretch pants and T-shirt. She eased a dark beanie over her red wig and fitted on a pair of gloves. Then she fished under the bed for her shoulder bag.

*What had Daisy meant about the message?* Jesse had no idea, but she would soon find out.

Jesse had memorized where everything was before

the light went out. Tracy told the truth when she said she had brought some of everything in her wardrobe. Right now, much of it was scattered over the carpet.

The door opened without a sound. Jesse peeked outside. The corridor was empty. A muffled cough came from the room opposite. *Jerome*. Ibrahim reckoned Jerome brought more medicines than clothes.

However, no light shone under doors and there was no hint of movement. Everyone was exhausted from all that running, stumbling and climbing earlier on.

As Jesse approached the landing, she heard a man and a woman talking quietly. *Uh oh*. She paused and peeked around the corner of the L-shaped landing. Tahlia and Bob, still in tracksuits, only red this time, sat on the bottom stair. A wide shaft of light from the games room lit up a rectangle of floor between the bottom stair and the front door.

Tahlia and Bob held drinking mugs. Jesse sniffed the air. Coffee, with full-cream milk. Naughty at this time of night. But maybe it was decaffeinated.

Jesse had a bigger problem than staying awake at night. She couldn't wait till they moved. Daisy would soon be at the summer house.

She thought quickly. Windows? No good. The ground floor was blocked. The window in her room was high and there were no trees close enough at that end of the house for her to climb on to. Besides, it might wake Tracy. It was a big risk to enter any of the other bedrooms.

*If you can't go down, go up.* That motto had worked for Jesse before. Earlier that day, when she first saw Peter on the landing, she had noticed a skylight above his head. There was a bolt on it, and hinges, so it should open.

It was dangerous. One slip and she'd be caught. But what other option was there? If she made a mistake, she could tell Tahlia and Bob she was playing a trick on them. Although the items in her shoulder bag would be hard to explain.

Nimbly, Jesse climbed on to the railing. With her eyes, she measured the distance to the architrave around the skylight. It was thick and looked solid. She couldn't quite reach. She'd have to jump, hang on with one hand, and slide the bolt with the other. *Great. I should have done my project on monkeys.*

She bounced a little, preparing her knees for action. *One. Two. Three!* Jesse took a deep breath and sprung upward. Her fingers connected with the architrave, curled around it, held on. There was a groove, which made it easier to grip. She steadied herself, then let go with her right hand. The physical training at C2 was relentless, but right now Jesse was thankful for it.

Her full body weight dragged on her left arm.

It ached immediately, as though a heavy rock was attached to her feet. Suddenly she had sympathy for the insects that carried fifty times their own body weight.

It was the same as an adult lifting two heavy cars.

Moving swiftly, while her arm would still support her weight, she drew back the small bolt on the skylight. *Please don't be nailed shut.*

There was a crack as it pivoted back on its hinges.

"Did you hear that?" Tahlia's voice echoed up the stairway.

Bob grunted. "Hear what?"

"I'd better check the corridor."

Adrenalin made Jesse's heart pound. She had only a few seconds before she was discovered.

# 21

*Phew. That was close.* Jesse sat on the roof near the skylight. Slowly, she breathed in and out a couple of times, then flexed her arms. Her biceps would be sore tomorrow.

Jesse peered down to the landing below.

Tahlia returned. She shrugged.

Jesse lip-read Tahlia's comment to Bob, "It was nothing."

Jesse's eyes adjusted quickly. She had better night vision than the average person. She could distinguish shapes and textures. A half moon was rising, and the stars were bright.

She stood and headed for the back of the house. Light filtered outside from the corridors and games room. Unlikely anyone would be in the kitchen at this hour. It didn't take long to find a branch that was close to the gutter and strong enough to hold her weight.

Then Jesse saw something that made her pause. A light in the garden flicked in and out of the bushes. Someone was out there with a torch. The dogs were not due to be let out for an hour. Tahlia and Bob were inside the house. Daisy would never use a light like that. It would draw attention. Mistakes could get you killed.

*Too late to stop the meeting now. I'll just have to be extra careful.* Jesse clambered down a huge old elm tree. *Ouch.* A twig stuck in the leg of her stretch pants. Grumbling, she stopped to free it, then continued.

She landed softly on the ground and, at a half-run, put distance between her and the house. Surrounded by bushes and trees, she was soon in the dark.

The sweet scent of roses told her the summer house was close.

There it was, black against the starry sky.

Jesse stopped, listened. There was no sound. She checked behind her, left and right. No sign of that light. She pushed open the door and stepped inside.

A second later, she caught the smell of lemon. It wasn't a natural aroma, but man-made.

The open door was pushed back at her, knocking into her side. She staggered.

An arm wrapped around her from behind. A hand pressed against her mouth.

Jesse let her knees sag. Her weight and the sudden crumpling of her body put her assailant off balance. He fell forward, against her back. She reached behind with her one free arm, grabbed his shirt and tugged. At the same time, she bent forward in one smooth movement, heaving the man over her head. He landed heavily.

Before he had time to catch his breath, she snatched a small tube from her shoulder bag and held it to his neck. "Don't move. One spray from this and your brain will be scrambled. You'll be talking backwards for the rest of your life."

A chuckle came from the man on the floor. "Not bad, little Operation IQ."

She recognised the voice instantly. Daisy. Or was it George tonight? He had abandoned the dress and body padding. In the dim light she saw he was thin again and wearing trousers.

"I've never heard of a spray that interrupts brain function."

"I didn't say you could get up." Annoyed with him, she pressed the tube harder to his neck. "Go on then, move. Let's test out the spray and see who's right."

"Come on," he said. "We work for the same people."

Reluctantly, she stepped back and slipped the tube into her bag. She'd never heard of a brain scrambling spray either. It would only have rendered George unconscious for a short time. But he didn't need to know that. "Why did you grab me?"

"To make sure it was you." George stood up and rubbed his neck. "To test your reflexes. Didn't anyone teach you to check behind open doors?"

"Didn't anyone tell you not to let girls throw you to the floor and threaten to make you unconscious?"

"OK. Fair enough. We were both careless. But be warned, if we meet again, I'll be a step ahead of you."

"Dream on." *From now on, the backs of doors and me are the best of friends.*

"Tell me about the message," she said.

He unzipped his jacket and took out something that looked like a hand-held scanner an airport security guard might use. "As I said in the kitchen, you have it."

"No one gave me any message."

She glimpsed teeth flashing as he grinned. "You carry

it. It's encoded in your DNA. It's *inside* you."

That's what all the whispering was about between Director Granger and Ari in the infirmary. What else had they done without telling her? They had no right. Not without her permission. She wasn't a person to them. Just an experiment.

"What's it about?" she asked.

"Nothing to do with you," he said. "You're just the carrier." He laughed. "You'll need to keep still while I scan your DNA sequence. Then you can go."

Jesse felt a wave of uneasiness. Could she trust him? It seemed rather personal to let him scan her DNA.

"Don't look so disapproving. I already have a copy of your DNA string. Whatever is extra is the message, which I'll decode."

"You'd better finish before the dogs are let loose. Or I'm out of here."

Outside, there was an unnatural rustle of leaves.

George stepped closer and whispered, "Were you followed?"

"Of course not. I'm a prodigy. I'd know if I was being followed."

"You didn't know I was behind the door."

*Good point.* "I thought I saw a torch light earlier. But I didn't see anyone when I came through the garden."

George pressed the scanner into her palm. His breath

smelled of coffee as he whispered, "Wait here."

He exited the summer house, quickly and quietly.

Then came what sounded like the snap of a twig, then a louder crack. Someone grunted. There was a thump.

*What's going on out there? Something's wrong.*

She felt along the bench beside her and located the nearest pot plant. With her fingers, she dug a hole, put the scanner in, then covered it over. If she was captured, no one would find it.

Cautiously, she left the summer house, creeping in the direction that George had gone. She dare not call out his name. Someone else might answer.

A bird in a nearby tree cried out, a sign that it had been disturbed. Jesse headed that way.

She spotted him quickly, lying on the ground, a darker blob against mottled foliage. She checked all round, but detected no other presence.

Jesse sank to her knees beside George. His head and half his face were unnaturally dark. *Blood.* The smell of it was distinctive. She felt for a pulse. There was none. Her hands touched his chest. It didn't move. She held her fingers in front of his nostrils. No air.

An acrid taste rose in her throat.

She didn't need to do the pen down the throat or the rag over the eyeball tests to know that George was dead.

Jesse shivered and looked around her in a wide circle. Did someone know about the message George was collecting tonight? She carried it. If someone was after that, then they were after her.

Who had done this to George, and why? Someone from Nimbus, C2, or a resident at the camp? It could have been someone entirely different. A burglar. But what was worth stealing from a rickety old summer house?

*Poor George. What am I going to do with you?*

She checked her watch. Tahlia or Bob would let the dogs out soon.

*I can't leave you out here with a pack of half-starved dogs patrolling the gardens. I can't bury you. Even if I had a shovel, which I don't, it would take hours.*

She couldn't report his death to Tahlia. How could she explain why she had climbed out of the skylight at night and found the housekeeper, Daisy, who was really a man called George and a secret agent for an organization no one had heard of?

If anyone in the house knew, that would undo her cover. The child with "abilities beyond normal" would know who she was. A horrible thought hit Jesse. *Could a child have done this?*

Her mind ran through stored facts. There were vulnerable areas on a human skull. One blow there could kill. A child could do it. Around the world 300,000 children were fighting in wars. It happened every day. But it was so personal, and callous, to smash someone's head in.

It was time to call for backup. Jesse messaged Liam, using her watch communicator.

She bent to touch George's shoulder. *Sorry to leave you alone. Liam will be here soon.*

At the other end of the garden dogs barked.

It was only a short walk back to the summer house, where she was to meet Liam. She pushed the door open, this time remembering to check behind it.

Instantly, the hairs on the back of her neck prickled.

There was no one behind the door, but someone else was in the summer house. Mingled with the odour of damp potting soil and mould, she detected sweat. And fear.

*OK, dude, unless you're wearing night vision goggles, I can see better than you. And I can smell you. That gives me the advantage.*

Quietly she eased past the bench with its line of pot plants. *Is that breathing I can hear?* Part of her wanted to turn and run, but she couldn't do that. If this was George's killer, then she had to get him. *Him? Yes. Him.* She couldn't say why, but she was certain that whoever was in the summer house with her was male.

*What if he has a weapon?* Her heart thumped painfully against her ribs. If he intended to kill her, he would have done so when she entered.

Her fingers slipped around the knockout spray. *What every girl needs.*

Her eyes picked out a darker, denser shape hunched down behind a large bag of fertilizer. Treading softly, she moved around the edge of the summer house, closer to the dark shape.

Before she could strike, the intruder hurled something at her. Automatically she turned her head aside and held her arms up for protection. It hit her forearm, then clattered to the floor. *Ouch. A metal trowel.*

He scrambled to his feet and bolted for the door.

Jesse dived forward and tackled his legs. He fell, kicked madly. One foot caught her on the side of the face.

*Right. I'm getting mad now.* Jesse scrabbled closer,

and pinned him, face down, to the floor with one knee. Then she twisted his arm up behind the shoulder blade. "One more degree of rotation and your shoulder blade will snap," she said, hoping he would lie still. She didn't want to follow through with her threat.

She aimed the tube at the side of his face and pressed.

He made a strangled sound as the spray hit him. His body sagged.

Jesse moved away a little, then prodded his arm. It was as limp as cooked spaghetti. She listened to his breathing. *Definitely unconscious.*

His face was turned away from her, but the shape of his head was familiar.

*Uh oh.* She grabbed one arm and flipped his unconscious body over, face up. Moonlight streamed in the windows, highlighting features she knew well. *Peter Keaton.*

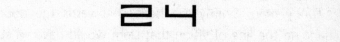

# 24

Jesse grabbed Peter's ankles and dragged him across the rough summer house floor.

Liam would be here any minute. She knew she should tell him about discovering Peter hiding in the summer house. But she couldn't do it. Not till she had a chance to talk with Peter, find out what he was doing here.

Instinct persuaded her to protect him. But was it right? Just because he had Rohan's face, and voice – if you discounted the stutter – that didn't mean he had Rohan's mind or heart. He wasn't Rohan. Yet turning Peter in would be like betraying her brother.

Even as she rolled him under a bench, tucked his arms down by his sides and propped large pots and the bag of fertiliser in front of him, uncertainty grabbed her. *Is Peter the infiltrator from Nimbus? Am I protecting a murderer?*

Jesse felt hot and sweaty, yet chilled at the same time.

79

The dogs had stopped barking. What did that mean?

She heard a footstep outside the summer house door. Then silence. Her wrist communicator vibrated. A text message from Liam said, "Don't attack. I'm at the door."

*Funny man.* Swiftly she headed towards the door, changing the line of vision that Liam would have when he entered. Now he would be looking away from Peter, not towards him. Liam sometimes acted as though he was thick as a brick, but he wasn't.

Like her, Liam was dressed in black. His body seemed to be absorbed into the half-darkness. Moonlight picked up his paler skin, making his head seem disconnected.

He closed the door and took a few steps inside. "Are you OK?"

"I just found a dead body. How could I be OK?"

"But you're not injured?"

"No."

"Are you sure it's George?"

"Positive."

"What happened?"

"The dogs will be out soon," she said, desperate to get Liam outside. "Shouldn't we do something about George?"

Liam shook his head. "The dogs are taken care of." He raised one hand. "Don't start. They're drugged, not dead."

Jesse relaxed. There had been enough death in this garden for one night.

Her eyes slid sideways. A jolt of electricity ran through her. Peter's feet protruded from beyond the fertiliser bag. She edged further around, hoping Liam's eyes would follow her. His night vision was not as good as hers. So maybe Peter's feet wouldn't be visible to him. But she couldn't be sure.

"Come on," she said. "I'll show you where George is."

Liam didn't move.

From the corner of her eye, Jesse saw Peter's foot twitch. The spray was only short-lasting. If he woke up now, Liam might take Peter back to C2. Jesse didn't want to think about what they might do to him to extract information.

"What are you up to, Jesse?" said Liam.

"What do you mean?"

"I might not be a genius, but your voice is tight and your back is as stiff as a board. You're nervous."

"I just found a body with a whopping great hole in its head." Her whisper became angry, terse. "What did you expect?"

Jesse felt perspiration drip down her back.

"You're keeping something from me, Jesse Sharpe," said Liam. "I hope you know what you're doing."

# 25

"He was here, I swear it." Jesse's voice was only a whisper, but she wanted to shout.

"This garden's pretty overgrown. Are you sure you haven't made a mistake?"

Frantically, Jesse checked all around the area she had last seen George. "Look, that bush is flattened. That's where he fell."

Liam took a small torch from his pocket. He turned it on and held it low to the ground. There were spots of fresh blood on several leaves. "You're right. It seems that someone has moved the body."

Jesse felt a dart of relief. Peter couldn't have moved the body. He had been wrestling with her in the summer house. And now he was lying unconscious behind a stack of pots. But he could still be involved. He might have an accomplice.

"First Seahorse, then George," said Liam. "What's going on?"

Jesse crouched beside Liam. "Seahorse?" He had been the undercover agent who had filed the report about the threat at this camp. So he was dead too.

"Jesse, I'm not happy that you're in here on your own." Liam sounded genuinely concerned. "I shouldn't tell you anything … but … who knows what will end up being important?"

Jesse could smell Chinese food – fish with ginger – on his breath as he whispered.

"Seahorse was a double agent. He was with C2 for years, but recently he wormed his way into Nimbus. The outer circle only. They don't trust easily."

*Neither does C2.*

"Unfortunately, he died. Nimbus wanted to find out what he knew. So did we."

"Bit hard interrogating a dead guy."

Liam nodded. "Yes, that's why C2 wants to change that."

Jesse saw a picture forming. So many things she thought were random and unconnected were actually parts of the same story. "Seahorse is Professor Sawyer." Right now, back at C2, they were trying to repair cell damage using nanotechnology.

"He died before he could give us enough details

83

about the operation here. All I know is this child from Nimbus has some kind of weapon. Something new and dangerous. The threat is real. And not just to you or me personally."

"You mean a threat to the city?"

"Bigger."

"The country?"

"Seahorse thought this weapon was a threat to the entire world."

Jesse thought about Atlas, a figure in Greek mythology, who held up the whole sky by himself. Then she imagined Atlas dropping the sky because it was too heavy. *What if I can't find this kid?*

"So far they haven't been successful with Sawyer, Seahorse, whatever you want to call him. Time is running out. Despite this hiccup with George, you have to go back in there."

*Hiccup? An odd way of describing murder.*

"So if I can't stop this kid, we could all die?"

"Seahorse was experienced. Seen everything. But he was rattled."

"And Dr Freeman?"

"*So you did* see that newspaper headline. I suspected you had." Liam shrugged. "His death could really have been an accident. But gut instinct tells me that Nimbus was furious that we stole Sawyer's body from under their noses. They might have blamed Freeman. You can't just freeze a body for re-animation any old place. It has to be done properly. That's why they put Sawyer in Cryohome. But any weak links that might lead people back to Nimbus had to be destroyed. That included Freeman."

If Peter was involved, Jesse knew she'd have to turn him over to C2. *Please don't let it be him.*

"Go back," said Liam. "But be careful. It's too late to send in someone else. It's up to you."

"Does this mean you don't want anything to happen to me?"

"It's too much trouble breaking in a new partner."

"Huh."

"And then there's Locard's principle."

*Locard's principle. When two things touch, they exchange material. It was a principle followed in forensic science.*

"I know you. Who else would nag me about my dirty car or my hair? I have to get out of here now. Stay strong."

*Great. Just when I look like making a friend, we might all die.*

# 26

Peter sat with his back propped against the bench in the summer house. "S-someone hit me."

"I did," said Jesse. "Although I didn't exactly hit you.

I just tackled you, kneed you in the back, twisted your arm, then sprayed you with a substance that made you temporarily unconscious."

"J-just?"

"Don't get mad with me," said Jesse. "You hit me first, with that metal trowel, and kicked me in the face." She ran a hand along her jaw. "Bet I get a bruise."

"Are you following m-me?" His voice was groggy.

"No. I didn't even know you were in the summer house." She sat directly in front of him, legs crossed like a toddler at kindergarten. "What are you doing in here?"

He looked away.

There wasn't time to muck around, drawing out information from Peter. *If it's him, I want to know. Now.*

"A man called George was murdered just outside the summer house about an hour ago," she added.

He flinched. It was immediate and instinctive. Jesse didn't think anyone could fake that good a reaction. "M-murder?" He sounded scared. "It wasn't me. I d-don't even s-spray s-spiders. I c-carry them outside to give them a fair chance to get away."

*That's exactly the sort of thing Rohan would do.*

"Anyway, what are you d-doing out here?" asked Peter.

Jesse made a decision to trust him. She hoped it was the right one. "I'm trying to save the world."

"You d-don't have to tell me if you d-don't want to."

*Why does no one believe me when I tell the truth?*

Peter sighed. "I w-was going to leave the c-camp for a few hours. But I got lost. Then I heard footsteps so I hid in here."

They were both silent for a moment. The footsteps could have belonged to the murderer.

"Where's the d-dead man?" asked Peter.

"I don't know. His body was stolen."

"S-stolen?" Peter's voice rose with shock.

"Ssh. Whisper. Why were you leaving?"

He shifted position, uncomfortable with her questions.

"Please tell me the truth. It's important. You could be in really big trouble. We all could."

"I've g-got a headache."

"And you're giving me one. Come on. Where were you going?"

"To visit a f-friend." He ran a hand through his hair but the fringe flopped back down again immediately. "I d-don't know what to do. I can't do this on my own any m-more."

"I know how you feel."

He sniffed again. "D-do you think promises are important?"

"Yes."

"B-but what if you m-made a promise not to tell a secret? But then you realize that if you don't b-break that promise, someone will d-die."

"If breaking the promise helps someone, then I think it would be OK. Besides, sometimes we don't know all the facts or we make a mistake. Let me help you."

"I'm looking after s-someone who's s-sick. Really s-sick." He faltered. "I think he might d-die."

"Who?"

"M-my brother."

Jesse and Peter stood on the footpath as the taxi drove away. They began to walk towards the ramshackle shed at the back of a vacant block not far from Peter's house.

*Thank you, Liam,* thought Jesse. She had a special bank account for expenses now that she had more freedom. But if Liam knew how she was using the money tonight, his hair would go white.

She checked her watch. *One a.m.* Everyone would be asleep back at camp. She had a little time. Besides, this might be her only chance to locate Rohan. If she let it pass, she might never see him again. And if he was half as sick as Peter insisted, he might die. This time for real.

"How were you going to get over here?" she asked. "You would have been walking all night."

"I have a b-bike, hidden in the garden," said Peter.

She looked over at the shed. Her heart pounded hard

enough to burst out of her chest. *Is Rohan really in there? So close?*

Jesse wanted to dash inside immediately. Yet she also wanted to delay. Another disappointment would be unbearable. Her hopes had gone up and down like a roller coaster.

Jesse was full of questions for Peter. They couldn't talk in the taxi. The driver was too curious about a boy and a girl going across town at night by themselves. Jesse had spun an involved story about a car accident, grandparents, and a father who was in jail. Although she thought the part about the flesh-eating disease was probably a bit much.

She checked left, right, and behind. *If Peter is the Nimbus infiltrator, this could be a trap.* He appeared believable, truthful. But so did she.

"How did you and your brother meet?" she asked.

"I was walking down the s-street and s-someone tapped me on the shoulder. I turned around and saw my own face. There was a b-boy, just like me."

"Bet you got a shock."

"I d-did. He told me he'd run away from some s-secret group. If they found him, they would kill him."

"You believed him?"

Peter shrugged. "He was really s-scared. He must b-be to live in this shed."

*He's not wrong. It looks as though it would fall down in a strong wind.*

"I s-sneaked him b-blankets and food from the house. He s-said to be careful. So I haven't told anyone about him. Till now. He was all right at first. But then he went funny. S-sick. I can't explain."

*You don't have to.*

Peter knocked on the shed door five times, two slowly, then three in succession. "If he knows it's me, he's not so s-scared." The door stuck a little, then gave way.

Jesse followed Peter inside. She wrinkled her nose. The inside of the shed was dark and musty. It smelt of old grass, sump oil and rotting food.

She flicked on her small torch. Over in the corner, wrapped in a blanket, was the shape of a body.

"He can't walk any more. S-sometimes he doesn't talk. But when he does, he s-says weird things. Numbers mostly."

Jesse remembered how her own brain had begun to scramble when her nanites broke down. She understood how it must be for Rohan.

She approached the shape wrapped in the blanket. As her torch beam highlighted his face, she gasped.

It was Rohan, but he looked dreadful. He was so thin his cheekbones looked set to break through his dry, yellow skin.

"He p-pulled out his eyelashes," said Peter. "Why would he do that?"

"He doesn't know what he's doing." She sat, before her legs collapsed. Her hands were shaking.

She didn't bother to offer Rohan the muesli bar she had in her pocket. He wouldn't be able to eat it.

Rohan's eyelids flew up. His fingers scrabbled, claw-like, at the top of the blanket. "Three," he babbled. "A snail can sleep for three years."

"I know," said Jesse. Gently, she slipped one hand beneath his head and lifted. Peter dribbled orange juice into Rohan's mouth. No one would notice one small bottle missing from the camp kitchen. Rohan swallowed some of the juice. Some rolled down his cheek. Jesse mopped at it with her sleeve.

Rohan focused on her face, blinked once or twice. "Women blink twice as fast as men. Jesse blinks twice as fast."

Beneath that madness, those storms she knew were exploding in his brain, he sensed it was her. Despite the red wig and green contact lenses. Perhaps he recognized her voice.

"He always talks about this J-Jesse."

She decided to go straight for the truth. "I'm Jesse."

Peter gaped.

"Ellie isn't my real name. Rohan and I grew up together."

"In that s-secret place?"

"Yes."

Peter grabbed her wrist. "You t-tricked me. I won't let you k-kill him."

She shook him off. "I would never do anything to hurt Rohan. *Never.*"

And yet, she could see only one way to make Rohan better. Take him back to C2 headquarters.

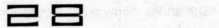

# 28

Breaking back into the old house at Watercress Camp was easier than breaking out. The dogs that Liam had doped were still quiet. *Snoring their bony heads off, probably.* Bob and Tahlia were gone from the stairs.

Peter gave Jesse a strange look as he disappeared inside his room. It was a mix of suspicion, accusation and relief all rolled into one.

That look cut her like a knife. She felt like a traitor. *What should I do?* She wished Jai was here. He was younger than both of them, and a little odd, but he was strangely wise. Rohan would die if she didn't take him back to C2. Yet how would he feel if she did? Would he hate her for it? Maybe he would rather be dead than go back there. She had promised Peter she wouldn't do anything tonight. Tomorrow she'd have to make a decision.

Peter had talked about going home, not returning to the camp, but they both decided that it would take explanations they were not prepared to give. All he had to do was stick it out for one more day.

*If I don't get a few hours' sleep, I won't be able to think clearly. About anything.*

Another door opened.

*Doesn't anyone sleep around here?*

Jerome stumbled out, coughing.

"What are you doing, Jerome?" She threw the question at him before he could ask her the same one. Sometimes the best defence was attack.

"I'm going to the bathroom."

"Me too," said Jesse.

"Why are you wearing your clothes?"

"Pyjamas are dorky."

"What's with the beanie?"

"I get a cold head at night."

Jerome coughed again. "What's that under your nail?"

Jesse looked down. Traces of George's blood were stuck under her thumbnail. Panic bubbled up inside her. She smothered it to answer in an even voice. "Had a bloody nose."

Jerome stepped back. "Uh. You might be contagious."

This kid had a real thing about germs. How did his parents persuade him to come to the camp without a troop of doctors?

"I need to wash my hands. And put on a fresh mask."

Tahlia might be right. Half of Jerome's problem could be oxygen deprivation. How could he breathe in enough air if he kept wearing those cotton masks?

Under the hall lights, perspiration on his face glistened. His cheeks were flushed.

"My legs are aching," he said.

*Does he have to list every symptom every time he sees someone?*

"Probably from the running we did today. Running is a form of eccentric exercise. The muscles are forced to lengthen while trying to contract." She smiled. "Maybe you should exercise in the morning before your brain figures out what you're doing."

Jerome looked blank.

"That was a joke, Jerome," she whispered.

"Oh." He gave another hacking cough.

An echo cough came from behind another door.

*Maybe coughing is like yawning. If one person does it, then you have to do it too.*

"I feel sick." Jerome bolted for the bathroom.

*Someone should send that kid home. Someone should send us all home.* Wearily, she shrugged. *Except I don't have a home.*

## 29

"Ellie. Ellie." A voice pierced her consciousness. She struggled to open her eyelids. They felt heavy. *What's that smell?* Then it hit her. *Blood.* Her eyelids popped wide open.

Standing beside her bed, teeth exposed in a cheery grin, but eyes missing in blank sockets, was George. Blood oozed down his face.

Jesse's lips moved but no sound came out. She tried again, forced out words. "You're dead." Her voice was little more than a tight whisper.

"But I haven't got the message."

"Get away from me. You're not breathing."

"Neither is Seahorse, but that could change."

"You're not real."

"I know about the shed, Ellie. They shoot traitors in the army."

Something was wrong. George had called her *Ellie.*

He knew her name was really Jesse.

"Ellie." This time a female voice called her. A hand grabbed her arm. Again, her body felt heavy, as though it was weighed down by bricks. She struggled to open her eyelids. A guttural sound burst from her lips. She sat up, eyes wide open. Jesse peered at the figure by her bed.

"Are you all right?" asked Tracy. "You were talking in your sleep."

Jesse longed to rip off her wig and scratch madly at her sweaty scalp. "Sorry. I had a nightmare."

"You probably got too hot. Shall we open the window?"

"Good idea," said Jesse, knowing that all the fresh air in the world would not help her forget what she had seen in the garden.

She forced herself to relax. *Breathe in. Breathe out.* Gradually her muscles relaxed and sleep took over. But with sleep came dreams again. Sirens. Slamming doors. Voices.

Jesse woke several times, her mind hot and tormented. *What should I do about Rohan? Where's George's body? Is Peter the infiltrator? Who knows about the secret weapon?*

Finally, at four a.m. she gave up on sleep. Trying to rest was more exhausting than staying awake. There was too much on her mind. And too much to do. She touched her jaw where Peter kicked her. It was tender, but not too bad.

She looked across at Tracy, who was sleeping soundly. Jesse wondered what it would be like to be a normal kid, who didn't go out on secret missions dressed in disguise and with a fake name.

No one knew who Jesse really was. No one could. Because if someone knew all about her, C2 would see that person as a threat. And C2 eliminated threats. How was it possible to make friends, even for a short time, if the other person saw only a false identity, not the real person?

Jesse sighed, knowing what she had to do next, and not liking it. She slipped out of bed and tiptoed towards Tracy.

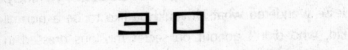

Smelly socks and the second-hand chewing gum were the worst things. Why would Grant keep old gum? Was he afraid there would be a worldwide shortage?

Then there was the sound in Priya's room – thumb sucking. *I'm not the only one with secrets. Bet she doesn't tell anyone about that.*

By the time Jesse had finished searching all the bedrooms, the sun was beginning to tint the horizon. One quick spray to each unsuspecting sleeper gave her uninterrupted time. Thieves used similar sprays on European trains. Once, on a trip to Germany, Liam had woken up with half an hour unaccounted for, and his wallet and watch gone.

Ibrahim had a mountain of chocolate bars hidden among his clothes. He shared a room with Jerome, who had enough medicines to start his own pharmacy.

Jesse didn't overlook anything. Methodically, she

worked her way down the corridor, room after room. She even opened each container of Tracy's makeup, wound up her lipstick and checked her three perfume bottles. Jesse was meticulous. If *she* could hide a camera in a lip balm tube and a laptop computer in her paint box, someone else could.

There was nothing that even hinted at a hidden weapon. Could C2 have been fed wrong information?

Reluctantly, she decided she might have to use her laptop to email photographs of the kids at camp to C2. She hadn't done it yet.

If she sent them, they would see Peter's face. She hadn't decided whether to turn Rohan in or not. For now, she had to keep Peter and Rohan secret from C2.

She considered keeping back that one photo and sending the others. But if Granger found out Peter was here and she had hidden it from him, he would demand to know why. Granger was capable of anything. Jesse shivered. *I can't think about that now. I have to find this weapon. It can't be in the house. I've searched. It must be hidden outside somewhere.*

Another thing puzzled her. Where was Jerome? His bed was empty. The last time she'd seen him, he was scuttling towards the bathroom.

She knocked on the bathroom door. "Jerome. Are you OK?" she whispered. There was no answer. She turned the handle. The bathroom was empty.

*Is he in the kitchen, getting a drink?* Torn between worry and suspicion, she crept downstairs.

She stopped suddenly at the kitchen door, surprised to find Tahlia and Bob sitting silently at the table.

"Jesse." Tahlia's eyes were red-rimmed, as though she hadn't slept much. She coughed, then swallowed hard.

She looked from Bob to Tahlia. They were both flushed.

"Is everything all right?" she asked.

"We don't want to spoil your weekend," said Tahlia, "but you'll wonder where Jerome is, so we might as well tell you straightaway. He was taken to hospital in an ambulance. He had a bad asthma attack. But the doctors think it's more than that. Some sickness triggered the asthma, but they're not sure what it is."

So the siren and banging doors hadn't been part of her dreams. They had been real.

"Jerome will be all right, though, won't he?" asked Jesse.

The silence was far too loud.

# ∃1

Tahlia looked at her watch. "Bob, should I wake the others or let them sleep in?"

Bob shrugged. He seemed physically smaller than he was when he strutted around yesterday. His hair, which yesterday had seemed shiny and luxuriant, was now limp and ratty. He gave a barking cough into his sleeve.

"It's hot in here." Tahlia crossed the room and opened the window.

A blast of cold morning air billowed inside. Jesse shivered. Then she heard the sound of a helicopter. More than one. And getting closer.

Bob looked up. "Must be an accident on the motorway."

Jesse felt her familiar warning prickle run across the back of her neck.

Cars pulled up outside, their tyres scrunching on the gravel driveway. Then a truck. Men in yellow hazard suits stormed past the window along the veranda.

*They're carrying guns,* thought Jesse.

"What's happening?" squealed Tahlia.

The door burst open.

A man barrelled into the kitchen. He was dressed in a hooded yellow hazard suit. A small window showed a white face with too many wrinkles on his brow.

Tahlia screamed.

Other people in hazard suits stood behind him.

He held up a badge. "By authority of the government, I am sealing this residence. No one may enter or leave. You will give us contact details for all parents. The children will remain here. Your phone lines will be cut. I expect you to hand over any mobile phones. The media must not be contacted."

*Terrific. How do I explain this to Granger?*

"Who are you?" shouted Tahlia. "Get out of this kitchen."

"I'm afraid I can't do that, ma'am. I'm Captain Tim Cross. Army doctor. I'm an expert in biological and chemical toxins."

"Chemicals?" said Tahlia. "Has there been a spill?"

"No, ma'am. The boy who was taken from here in the early hours of the morning was the victim of a virus."

"So?" Tahlia collapsed into a chair. "A cold is a virus."

Captain Cross directed an icy stare at her.

"Ma'am. Ebola is a virus. And HIV. A virus may be a

simple organism, but that only makes it more difficult to kill. That boy had a virus that no one has seen before. Our experts suspect it was genetically engineered."

Jesse's stomach turned cartwheels.

"The virus could have been spread in food, drink, or as a spray. We don't know yet. Nor do we know how to stop it. Until we contain the threat, no one leaves this building."

Suddenly it was clear to Jesse. Nimbus had a weapon that was too small to see. That weapon was a virus.

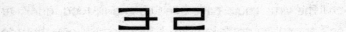

"I want to see my friend," said Jesse.

The woman in the yellow hazard suit outside Peter and Yingbao's room gave Jesse a penetrating look.

*Is she wondering why I'm not sick?* Jesse felt like a cactus in a pansy patch, the only one with no virus symptoms. She bent over and pretended to cough into her hands. She'd heard enough hacking coughs in the last few hours to mimic the sound precisely.

"Please," gasped Jesse. "This might be the last time I see my friend." It wasn't difficult to encourage a few tears that would make her eyes shine and her face pathetic. "Come on. We've both got the same virus, so we're not going to infect each other, are we?"

"All right. Be quick. You should be resting."

Jesse thanked her and entered Peter's room.

She knew that they would search her own room soon. Captain Cross's team had worked their way through most of the house sampling water, food, the air-conditioning system, the chimney, everyone's luggage.

They wouldn't find anything strange in Jesse's room. Not unless they lifted the blanket, sheet and mattress protector on her bed. While Tracy was asleep, Jesse had cut a small opening in the mattress with her pocket knife and hidden her gadgets inside it. Her wrist communicator was safe to keep. It looked like an ordinary watch.

Voices from the corridor billowed through the upper storey. "What do you mean you can't find her?"

*That's Captain Cross.*

The reply was quieter, mumbled.

"We have an army of people. How can we lose one housekeeper?"

*Easy. If that housekeeper doesn't exist.* They were looking for a plump woman called Daisy, not a thin man called George.

Jesse looked over at Yingbao. There was a drip in his arm. He was either deeply asleep or unconscious.

The virus had progressed more slowly with everyone else than it had with Jerome. He was asthmatic and had poor health. The virus had raged through his body like a speeding car in a Grand Prix. But, in only a few hours, the other patients had deteriorated. No one could leave the house, not even to go to a hospital. The army doctors brought their own medical equipment. "We can't risk the virus getting out."

The dogs no longer barked. Jesse asked no questions. She didn't want the answer.

Jesse knelt beside Peter's bed.

He looked familiar, so close to being family. Bright red splashes coloured his cheeks. Perspiration dotted his forehead.

*What if he dies? It's my fault because I couldn't find the weapon in time.*

"Peter." She touched his arm. "It's Ellie. Jesse."

He looked at her for two or three seconds before registering who she was. "It's hot in here."

"Do you want a drink?"

He nodded.

Jesse lifted his head and held a glass of water to his lips. "I have to talk to you. I've only got a few minutes."

"You're going to take Rohan b-back to that place, aren't you?"

"He'll die if I don't. The doctors there have special treatments that no one else has. They fixed me. They can fix Rohan."

Peter's voice was fading. She leaned closer to hear his reply.

"If they d-do this treatment thing, will he be normal?"

"He's never *normal*. But he'll be well. And alive."

Peter blinked slowly.

"Anyway," said Jesse. "What's normal? These kids at the camp are supposed to be normal. But they're all weird."

Peter's eyes showed he agreed.

"I don't think there is such a thing as normal," said Jesse. "Everyone's weird. Or at least, we're just ourselves. Normal sounds like being part of a group where you all have to be the same. Rohan will be … himself."

Peter coughed.

She waited till he was quiet again. "I want you to say it's OK for me to look after him. You're Rohan's family."

Peter gave a small nod. "So are you."

She swallowed with difficulty. "I have to go now."

"After you go b-back, will I see you b-both sometimes?"

"I don't think so. It could put you in danger. Maybe one day…"

Peter's eyes closed. He was still breathing. But for how long?

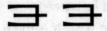

# 33

*I have to get out of here.* Jesse leaned her forehead against the window in the bedroom she shared with Tracy. The veranda below blocked her view. Guards in yellow hazard suits were stationed on the edge of the lawn and there were more outside the doorways. *It would be safer if it was dark. But I can't wait that long.*

Escape was going to be tricky. She couldn't fight the whole army. But she had one advantage. The medical staff believed all the children were too sick to leave.

Soon, Captain Cross and his staff would realize that she was not sick. They would want to know why. Already, they looked at her too intently, whispered so that she couldn't hear. Jesse could fake symptoms, but she couldn't fake a temperature or other effects of the virus.

Captain Cross and his team could not find the source. Yet everyone but Jesse was sick. Now the blood tests would start. Jesse couldn't let them do that to her. They would find evidence of the nanites that enhanced her abilities.

From one of the other rooms came a loud cry. Several sets of feet ran towards it.

Jesse leaped back into bed, dragging the covers over her head. *Uh oh. Who's in trouble?*

The blanket created a cocoon. It surrounded and hid her. Suddenly a shocking idea hit Jesse. *I know where the virus is hidden.* It was blindingly clear. *Why didn't I think of it before?*

She remembered the story of the Trojan Horse. The Greeks gave a huge wooden horse to the Trojans as a gift. The horse was towed inside the gates of the city. Then, Greek soldiers who were hidden inside the horse burst out. The Trojans were beaten.

*If the nanites are inside a body, maybe that's where the virus is hidden. Inside a body. Just like the soldiers were inside the giant horse.*

Jesse pictured the faces of all the children at Watercress Camp. The Nimbus child didn't have a secret weapon. He or she was a secret weapon.

# ∃ㄐ

Jesse knelt on the roof and, sheltered by a chimney, checked out the position of the guards.

She had a plan. Now she had to make it work.

Liam had received her message. He would be waiting by the back fence to whisk her away. The hard part would come after that. *One step at a time. Don't think too far ahead. You'll scare yourself.*

Jesse adjusted her backpack. All her belongings, including her smaller shoulder bag, were inside it. Then she climbed down from the roof on to the branches of the old elm tree. *This is getting to be habit.* Half-hidden among the thick lime-green leaves, she waited.

A guard in a yellow hazard suit, rifle tucked under his arm, sauntered underneath. He didn't look up.

He was too tall, so she let him pass.

*This one looks better.*

A shorter guard approached. A woman.

Hurriedly, Jesse checked that no one was watching. Then she jumped. Her feet caught the guard in the back.

The guard's head thumped the ground hard. She didn't move.

*Sorry.* Jesse grabbed the woman's shoulders. *It's not personal. I knock everybody out.* She dragged the unconscious guard behind the thick trunk of the elm tree into the wood shed. Jesse groaned as she straightened. *I have to give up moving bodies. They're too heavy.*

Jesse's fingers felt stiff and awkward as she undid the woman's yellow hazard suit. She shouldn't contract the virus out here in the open air, and Jesse needed a disguise. Her fingers wouldn't move as fast as her brain commanded. But it didn't take long. Clad in the borrowed suit, her face concealed by the hood, Jesse resumed the patrol around the gardens. She held the rifle under one arm, precisely as the woman had done.

By the time her friends found a woman in T-shirt and army trousers with her hazard suit missing, Jesse would be gone. Briefly, she crossed her fingers for luck.

She tensed as another figure came towards her. He nodded. She nodded back and kept walking. If she had to talk, it would be her voice that would give her away.

Past the edge of the lawn, the rhododendrons and the yellow poppies. She was almost to the back of the estate, where Liam would be waiting.

A bullet shot past her head and embedded itself in the tree trunk beside her. Jesse veered sideways, put on some speed. A quick check over her shoulder showed two soldiers in pursuit.

She ditched the rifle into a bush. Its weight slowed her down. Then she ran.

Director Granger sat behind his desk and raised one eyebrow. "Would you repeat that?"

Jesse knew that he had heard her perfectly the first time. "I need to go back to Watercress Camp."

"But we just got you out."

*No kidding. I was shot at, scraped the skin off my arms getting over the wire fence and was then hosed down by Liam in case I was contaminated. Yes, I think I remember that.*

"I want to find out who the carrier is," Jesse told Granger. "I still don't know."

"That's unfortunate."

"It all happened so fast. This child could go on spreading the virus if we don't stop it."

He said nothing.

"If Jerome hadn't had asthma, it would've taken longer to notice everyone was sick with the same symptoms."

It was weird. If Nimbus had wanted to kill lots of people, there were quicker ways to do it.

"We can cure them, Director. My nanites have kept me healthy. Ari checked. I'm fit. No trace of the virus.

I can break back in and inject them all with nanites," said Jesse. "Ari could programme them just to fight the virus. Nothing else."

Granger rested his fingertips on his chin. "We can't do that."

Jesse felt as though he had slapped her. "Why?"

"We can't risk our technology falling into the wrong hands. What if all this is a test to see whether we have a means of fighting it?"

"A test?"

"Jesse. Infecting a small group of science students is on too small a scale to be a serious attack."

"But another few hours and those kids would have gone home and infected their families."

Granger shrugged.

"What kind of people would test a bio-toxin on children?"

Jesse didn't like the expression in his eyes. Had C2 done the same thing? Whether they had or not, Granger was willing to let the kids at camp die.

"That virus is deadly," she tried again to persuade him. "It could spread all over the place. Even here."

"Hardly. We have an antidote. The nanites."

"But you won't share it?"

He leaned forward. "In any struggle there is collateral damage. You aim at one thing and hit another. It can't be helped."

"Twenty people are dying."

"I didn't make them sick. Blame Nimbus. If they set a virus loose, then you can bet they have a vaccination or an antidote themselves."

"But they wouldn't give us the antidote."

"Neither will I."

"If you know how to stop it and you don't, then aren't you as bad as they are?" She heard the tension in her own voice, the increase in volume.

"Remember who you're talking to, miss. I suggest you forget all about this matter."

"What about George? Someone killed him."

"George died for his country. We can be proud of him." Granger stood.

"There is one more thing." Jesse felt sick. Granger in a good mood was scary. What would he be like in a rage? But she was not going to let this go.

"Here is the biggest reason why I think we should help those kids." She put a photograph on Granger's desk.

All colour drained from his face.

# ∃ᴲ

Jesse shambled along the house corridor in the yellow hazard suit. It crackled and rustled, as though every action was being advertised. She looked down at the floor.

Shrouded in yellow, faces covered by hoods, the medical staff looked like identical aliens.

"Got the late shift?" Someone asked her.

She nodded. If her heart thumped any louder, everyone would hear it.

"You doing the temperatures?"

Again, Jesse nodded and turned her head half-aside, as though she was distracted.

"That girl, Ellie, hasn't been recovered either. The Captain's furious. Wants her back dead or alive. Judging by his mood, I'd say he'd prefer dead."

*Thanks for nothing.*

Jesse entered Peter's room. He was still breathing. So

was Yingbao. But they looked worse. Yesterday, Peter was stocky and physically strong. In only a day, he seemed shrunken. The distinctive flush on his cheeks had gone, leaving his skin yellowish and waxy.

*You first.* She pushed up Peter's sleeve and injected him. Then Yingbao.

Gradually, she worked her way down to the room she had shared with Tracy. *One to go.*

Tracy lay on her side, eyes closed, curled into a half-circle.

Jesse had the syringe ready.

Tracy stirred, moved her head. Her eyes were mere slits. Then, suddenly, they sprang open as she realized that it was Jesse's face behind the shield.

"What are you doing?" Tracy's voice sounded surprisingly strong.

"I'm going to make you better."

Abruptly, Tracy swung her free arm around like a windmill blade and grabbed Jesse's wrist. The syringe dropped on the carpet.

Jesse gasped. A flash of movement came a second before something heavy hit her on the side of the head. She fell sideways, struck the chest of drawers, then collapsed on to the floor. She lay there, confused and shocked. Even if she had wanted to move quickly, she couldn't. The heavy hazard suit made it impossible.

Tracy leaped from the bed, grabbed a thick book from her bedside table and dropped it on the syringe. She locked the bedroom door, then dragged a storage chest across it.

Jesse couldn't stop her. Her vision was blurred and her head spun. Furtively, she managed to press a button on her wrist communicator. The gloves made her hands awkward, but she only needed to press once. Liam knew what it meant.

A trail of dead bodies littered the plans of Nimbus. Professor Sawyer, Dr Freeman and George. Add to that a house full of children infected with a deadly virus. *And I'm trapped inside a body suit, in a locked room, with the maniac who's responsible.*

# 37

"There's no way out of here," Jesse told Tracy. "You might as well give up." She knew it was a pathetic threat, but it was all she could think of. Her side ached where she had hit the drawers.

"I know." The soft whine that had been in Tracy's voice yesterday had vanished. "I'm not going anywhere, so it doesn't matter. But neither are you. You can't give any more injections."

Jesse didn't tell her that she was the last. They had all been vaccinated, even Bob and Tahlia.

"You're the weapon," said Jesse, struggling to sit up.

Tracy looked at her as though she saw something curious, interesting, but nothing to get too excited about. "Who are you? Why aren't you sick?"

"Just lucky, I guess."

"Nobody's that lucky. You're from C2, aren't you?"

The door handle turned as someone outside tried to

open it. A muffled voice came from the corridor. "Why is this door locked?"

"I wondered about you," Tracy said to Jesse, ignoring the sounds outside the bedroom. "You were gone for hours last night. I thought you were meeting your stuttering boyfriend. Need a hand to get up?"

"No. I like it down here." She wasn't letting that girl touch her, even through the body suit.

Tracy shrugged.

"If we're both stuck in here, you might as well tell me – why a virus?" said Jesse. "Why not just throw a hand grenade or drop a bomb?"

A smile revealed Tracy's pink braces. "It doesn't matter now. It's almost over for all of us. So I'll tell you. The virus is genetically engineered to target a specific group. They were meant to take it away with them before they showed symptoms."

There was a variety of nationalities and backgrounds here. Yet, apart from Tracy and herself, they all had the virus. "What group?"

"Children. It's brilliant really. If you want to reduce pesky bird populations you destroy the nest and the eggs. It's the same with humans. And it's difficult to find who's to blame for a virus."

"Don't you care that all these people are sick?" Jesse felt her face grow hot with anger.

"No." Tracy smiled again. She looked like an ordinary, pretty girl. But that face hid the mind of a murderer. "I don't have feelings. My friends didn't activate the areas of the brain that produce emotions. I was genetically engineered to share viruses. I do my job without emotions getting in the way."

"That's awful."

"Is it? How many feelings do you have that you don't like?"

Jesse didn't answer, but there were a few.

More knocking came at the door, then louder voices. "Open this door. What's going on in there?"

"How can you tell what's right or wrong if you can't feel anything?" said Jesse.

"Makes it easier to do as I'm told. Because I don't care. I *can't*. Just as well. I'm going to die soon."

"But the virus hasn't made you sick."

Tracy shrugged. "My body mimics the symptoms. But no, I am not sick. My friends engineered a short life for me. I do my job, then I disappear. But that's all right. Someone will replace me."

Jesse's stomach turned. This girl was born to kill other people, and she didn't care. And yet Tracy couldn't help being twisted. She had no choice in what they did to her. Just like Jesse.

"Why did you kill George?" asked Jesse.

"Was that the man in the garden? He saw me."

"What did he see you doing that was so important?" asked Jesse.

Whatever Tracy was doing out there, she wasn't going to say. She put up her feet and settled back against the pillows. "There is always a price to pay. But we're moving towards the light."

"What light?"

Captain Cross's voice bellowed from the corridor. "We're going to break down the door." Axes splintered wood. Voices rose in a jumble of instructions and threats.

"You don't know what the light is, do you, Tracy?" asked Jesse. "You're repeating what they told you."

"Don't you?"

# 38

Jesse looked out through the open door of the ambulance. It was probably her last glimpse of Peter. His mother would be pleased to see him back home. The homes in Peter's street had straight garden edges, trimmed hedges and nicely painted gutters. It was not the kind of suburb you would expect to deliver a boy who almost died from a deliberately planted virus. Nor would anyone suspect that a boy would hide his sick twin brother in a grotty shed in case secret agents came looking for him. If these people knew the truth they would have a few sleepless nights.

At first Jesse liked Peter because he resembled Rohan. Now she liked him for keeping Rohan alive, and just for being himself. Once again, Peter had saved Rohan. And the other kids at the camp. Thanks to Peter's photograph, Granger couldn't resist intervening.

She looked across at the small scanner she had

retrieved from the summer house. She'd give a lot to know the message that C2 had stored in her DNA. They hid a lot from her. Jesse shrugged. *I guess it's not that important. I'm alive, I have Rohan back and I'm not going to stop trying till we're all free.*

Liam returned to the ambulance from Peter's house with an empty gurney. He looked more respectable in a uniform, although there was always a hint of wildness about him. "Peter is safely home. He'll be OK."

"Thanks."

"You owe me."

"I thought we were even," she said. "I've saved your life a couple of times now."

"Hah!" Liam looked outraged. "If Granger knew what I've done, I'd be taking a long walk off a short jetty."

"You were almost too late. Need a battery for your watch?"

Despite their own hazard gear, the C2 team had waited for Jesse to inject each patient then give the all-clear before bursting into the house. Even for this, Granger wouldn't risk his own people becoming infected. "If you manage to vaccinate all the sick ones, I'll send in a team," he'd promised.

Nobody knew then that the virus was aimed at children. The nanites had done their job and had been flushed out. The patients' recovery had been so quick that even Jesse was surprised. Each child had been sent home to recuperate.

Today, Captain Cross's team would retreat, puzzled at the sudden disappearance of the strange virus and the blank in their own memories. It seemed that C2 had a drug for everything. Even one that caused short-term amnesia. Jesse wondered what sort of minds those laboratory scientists had, to invent all these things.

"Do you think we could stop gassing and drugging people now?" she asked Liam. "I'm sick of it."

Liam looked over at Rohan, who was sleeping on a gurney. "So now I'm guilty of twin swapping. What next? It's a clever plan though. Peter's adoptive mother gets him back in one piece. Granger gets Rohan. And neither of them knows about the other boy. I'm glad we're on the same side. You're one scary agent."

Granger had seen a photograph of Peter and thought it was Rohan. It was a chance to reclaim an Operation IQ prodigy. Alive. And it wasn't Rohan's fault that his old nanites became corrupted, so he wouldn't be punished.

Liam shrugged. "I see why Granger didn't pick the difference in the two boys. They're like peas in a pod."

"Peter has eyelashes," said Jesse.

"So did Rohan, I presume. And he will again."

Jesse reached out and took Rohan's hand. He didn't seem to recognize her now. His eyes were open but his mind was shut. Yet his fingers tightened on hers. Maybe the warmth of another hand, a feeling of comfort, was enough.

She thought of Tracy. She was wrong about emotions. Not caring wasn't the way to promote your cause. Caring was. It was hard and sometimes it hurt. But if nobody cared, eventually people would wipe each other out. There would be nothing left.

She shuddered at the memory of how Tracy had aged in just a day. Skin like worn boot leather, fingers tightened into claws and her hair going grey overnight. Tracy's whole system collapsed. And she didn't care. That was almost the strangest part.

Liam had not been impressed. "She's useless for giving us information. But at least she can't contaminate anyone else."

Tracy was dead, but Nimbus could make other kids like her. They probably already had. *And I'll be ready.*

"Ari is the best in his field," said Liam. "He'll fix your friend."

"My brother." Jesse stroked Rohan's hand. "He's my brother."

If Ari could fix Rohan – and she was betting that he could – Rohan would wake to find himself back in C2, a place he loathed. Then he would discover that Jesse had brought him in. Would he hate her for it?

"What made you trust me to help, Jesse?" asked Liam. "Until now, I've had the distinct impression that you trusted me about as far as you could kick me. And, despite your supposed skill at tae kwon do, that wouldn't be far."

She had asked herself the same question. "Who said I trusted you? I always ask people I know to swap bodies in ambulances."

Jesse looked aside. What if, one day, Liam used this secret about swapping Peter for Rohan against her? She hoped that would not happen. Not just because it would mean trouble, and danger for Peter. But because it would hurt if Liam betrayed her. She did not trust easily. She couldn't afford to. Trusting the wrong person could be fatal.

Liam grabbed the handle of the ambulance door, ready to shut Jesse in the back with Rohan.

"I tell you one thing," said Jesse. "I've given up wanting to be normal."

"Just as well," said Liam, and closed the door.

Hello

I've sneaked out from C2 for a little while and my friend, Christine Harris, has now set up two email addresses for me:

jesse@christineharris.com
jesse@christineharris.com.au

You could also use the website link
www.christineharris.com/spygirl.html

Any secret communications should be safe on these addresses. I hope lots of readers will write to me after they read my books.

Jesse Sharpe, child prodigy and hamburger lover

Now that you have finished reading *Girl Undercover 3: Nightmare*, here is Chapter 1 of *Girl Undercover 4: Danger...*

# 1

Jesse's stomach lurched. Something was seriously wrong.

She stared at Liam, her C2 partner. The colour had drained from his face. His skin looked like wax. He jammed his mobile into his top pocket, turned the car key and gunned the engine. The car shot forward.

Jesse's head thumped back against the head rest. She looked down to check that her seat belt was fastened.

In seconds the car was doing the speed limit, then zoomed past it. Liam always said that the rust patches and dented bumper bar of his car hid a super motor.

He didn't lie, thought Jesse. He lies about nearly everything else. But not the car.

"Where are we going?" Jesse grabbed the bar above the door to steady herself. "I know our C2 assignments are top secret. But if I'm going to die, I'd like to know now."

She squealed as Liam slammed around a corner. A pedestrian leaped on to the footpath, shaking his fist.

Liam's shoulders were hunched, his eyes narrowed. "I'm going to pull over and let you out, Jesse. You can't be involved in this."

Her jaw dropped. This was a first. He hadn't shown this much concern on their last assignment, when they were stealing dead bodies. "Why? Did Director Granger tell you to do that?"

Liam was silent.

So Granger didn't give that order. "I'm staying," she said.

"This is serious, Jesse." Liam weaved in and out of traffic lanes like a mad man. "There are no other agents close and we only have ten minutes."

Jesse gasped as Liam ran a red light. Other drivers braked suddenly in terror and confusion. "Then you don't have time to drop me off. Every second counts. Besides, I won't let you go into a dangerous situation on your own. It's against the rules."

Liam snorted. "What do you care about rules?"

She shrugged. He was right. If she heard a rule she was tempted to break it. "I'm a kid. I'm supposed to hate rules." She took a deep breath. "Maybe I care about you. Anyway, I owe you from our last assignment. And you might need two people. Where are we going?"

"The underground."

"You want to catch a train?"

"No one would want to catch a train there right now. Not if they knew what could happen." He shook his head. "That call ... I've never heard that tone in Granger's voice. I think he was frightened." Liam's voice trailed into a whisper as though he couldn't believe his own words.

Hot pins and needles shot across the back of Jesse's neck. It was her warning sign, an instinct of approaching danger. Director Granger was an "ice man". Cold, ruthless, and he rarely revealed emotion. If Liam was right, and Granger was frightened, then something dreadful was about to happen.

Liam wiped perspiration from his top lip with his sleeve. "C2 just had a call from someone who says he's planted a bomb in the underground Central Station. Not just an ordinary bomb. It contains anthrax."

# CHRISTINE HARRIS

Spy Girl is Jesse Sharpe. Jesse is twelve years old.
She is a prodigy, a genius. She speaks five languages
and was reading encyclopedias at age three.
With other child prodigies she has been "adopted" by
a secret organization, C2, and is on assignment as part
of Operation IQ. Children can go where adults cannot,
and adults seldom notice them. But that doesn't make
Jesse's task any less dangerous…

Girl Undercover 1: Secrets
Girl Undercover 2: Fugitive
Girl Undercover 3: Nightmare
Girl Undercover 4: Danger

**Christine Harris** is one of Australia's busiest and most popular
children's authors. She has written more than thirty books as well
as plays, articles, poetry and short stories. Her work has been
published in the UK, USA, France and New Zealand.
www.christineharris.com